Into the Ruins

Issue 2

Summer 2016

Published July 2016 by Figuration Press

Into the Ruins is a project and publication of Figuration Press,
a small publication house focused on alternate visions of the future
and alternate ways of understanding the world,
particularly in ecological contexts.

intotheruins.com

figurationpress.com

ISBN 13: 978-0-9978656-0-8
ISBN 10: 0-9978656-0-1

Editor's Note:
In the case of international authors utilizing British English,
I have opted in both this issue and the first issue to keep their usage intact
rather than altering their spelling and grammar to American English standards.
This was a considered decision made in celebration of ideals of localization,
the themes of *Into the Ruins*, and the sort of futures I expect we face.
I hope the occasional shift in usage does not too annoy or frustrate readers,
and I appreciate your patience.

Comments and feedback always welcome at editor@intotheruins.com
Comments for authors will be forwarded.

Issue 2
Summer 2016

TABLE OF CONTENTS

Preamble

Stories

Reviews

Coda

PREAMBLE

NATURE-MADE FUTURES
BY JOEL CARIS

The other night I wandered outside my friends' house, situated along a rural highway a few miles inland on the north Oregon coast, surrounded by both darkness and the light of July's full moon. A noise that sounded to me like the best kind of silence carried through the air: a litany of frogs calling from a nearby slough in tumbling harmony. Of course it was a silence only in the sense of its familiarity as the audible and comforting backdrop to a place I love.

I miss that singing. Nearly three months ago, after publishing the first issue of *Into the Ruins*, I moved from the rural north Oregon coast back to the city—to Portland, to be exact. I had lived on the coast for five years, working for a succession of farms—both vegetable and animal—and then for a local nonprofit, my life changing dramatically during that time. I returned to Portland not due to a desire to leave the coast, but for the greater desire to live with someone I had fallen in love with and who had become the most important person in my life.

I know and like this city, Portland, but I also miss the frogs. I miss, too, the coyotes. That same night, back out on the coast, their yips and cries cut through the darkness late as I lay in bed, the window open to the nighttime air. I heard coyotes commonly while I lived out on the coast and, just as back then, their sudden and boisterous cries brought me delight. Even though they came regularly deep in the night during my time on the coast, the calls always surprised me in the best of ways.

In my experience, this is one of the primary gifts of the natural world: the ability to consistently surprise. Often this is in delightful ways, yet also often in painful ways. One of the great challenges with a project such as this magazine is that so much of our future lies not within the provenance of humans, but in that of the natural world around us and the multitude of overlapping ecosystems and natural phenomena that drives it. The results from that incomprehensibly complex system are often unknowable for us humans, outside the reach of our limited minds. As such, one of the few certain predictions I can make about our future is that it's bound to surprise all of us, though likely in different ways depending on the person.

The surprises can be so simple. Close to five years ago, during my first winter living out on the coast, I emerged from my yurt on a very frosty morning to tend to the farm's small flock of ducks. They needed out of their house for the day and they needed water. (Ducks, for those who might not know them, most always need water, for it seems to be their greatest joy in life.) After letting them out into the cold morning, I grabbed the stiff-with-frost hose lying on the ground next to the coop and cranked the water faucet on. For a moment, nothing. Then a tremor, the pressured gurgle of water, and a series of icicles spitting out of the hose, shattering at my feet on the rocky ground; a simple, unexpected, and delightful moment.

It was such a small occurrence borne of such a simple phenomenon: a bit of water remaining in the hose overnight, freezing not quite tight enough in the hose to come shooting out at the behest of new water under pressure. Yet this small surprise brought me significant joy, to the point that I remember it nearly five years on and it stands out as one of my happiest memories on the farm.

I believe that delight goes hand in hand with the surprise. The natural world is very good at creating realities that we can't foresee, and often those realities are arrangements of the physical world we never expected. Sometimes those arrangements will take the form of shattered icicles strewn across displaced river rock, bringing joy and delight. Other times it may be more unnerving, like wild weather fluctuations bespeaking an increasingly destabilized climate.

So often, when we speak of the future, it's about human arrangements—which are, of course, as natural as any other arrangement on this planet, but in a very limited way. We talk about human technology, our political and social and economic systems, current cultural realities, and the ways they may change. We speak about all the things we build and create—houses, cars, computers, gadgets, books, films, art, dinner, a quality beer, and so on. Sometimes we imagine how the non-human world may change, but even that is often centered around the ways we think it might change due to our actions. Our imagined futures most often start from the perspective of humans and with the assumption that human constructs are what are most important and pressing. Too often, the natural functions and the vagaries of the non-human environment—all the happenings, in other words, that ultimately most determine what our future will be, and that create the sort of diversity of realities that humans can only begin to imagine—are left out of the equation.

Moving back to Portland after having lived in a rural area helps to bring this home for me. Cities are the ultimate in human-built environments. They are scrubbed almost entirely of the wild. Depending on the city and the neighborhood, there may be a number of non-human life forms to be found—trees, native and ornamental plants, grass, gardens, pets, insects, and a wide variety of wild crit-ters—but even those have very often been situated and placed by humans, or are adapted wild animals who would exist in far less abundance or not at all if not for the human-built environment around them. Worse yet, a particular neighborhood may consist of little more than concrete, streets, buildings, and the utter extin-guishment of most everything non-human or uncontrolled by humans. This is the ultimate in human construct, and as John Michael Greer wrote in a series of fasci-nating essays[1] last year, such a landscape can significantly alter human thinking and the ways in which we understand and deal with the world. I might argue, as well, that it can diminish the amount of delight and surprise found in the world.

Now, in Portland, I'm lucky enough to live in a neighborhood brimming with trees and plants, alive with walkers and bikers and human activity, crawling with neighborhood cats and dogs, filled with birdsong and gardens, and otherwise quite pleasant as a place to live, even in some of the same ways as out on the coast. Much as the cries of the coyotes brought me joy a few nights ago, for instance, so too did the somewhat nonsensical but happy chatter of a toddler with his father some days before that, the two passing by outside our apartment and their voices carrying through the evening air and into our apartment via an open window. And yet, liv-ing here is quite different than living along a rural highway on the coast, where land abounds, building are infrequent, livestock dominates, and wild animals run far more abundant and free. Coyotes do not break the nighttime quiet here in Portland; sometimes it's the happy chatter of a toddler, but it's also often the not-as-delightful explosion of fireworks, grumble of cars, shouting of adults, clamor of parties, and blasting of music. Portland is a lovely place to live, but when those are the sounds coming through my window, I admit I miss the frogs. (Though they, too, can be found in Portland.)

Of course, the dichotomy is far less dichotomous than presented here. While land abounds out on the coast where I used to live, a significant portion of it has been intensely altered by humans, with forests and wetlands cleared long ago to create pasture for dairy cows and lumber for human use. Wolves do not roam out there; coyotes do. The vast majority of wolves, after all, were killed long ago. Occa-sionally you catch a glimpse of a black bear. It's rare. Cows outnumber humans in Tillamook County, but there were no cows there before humans. Most of the land is not covered in concrete, but that hardly means it hasn't been altered.

Yet there are not nearly enough humans out there to manage all that land with the intensity brought to bear on it during its initial taming. As time goes on, the wild begins to take back hold in ways that it far less often does in the city, muddling the human imprint and slowly seeding the landscape with new surprises. Ecosystems impose themselves, alter human efforts, and craft new realities unforeseen by us.

---

[1] http://thearchdruidreport.blogspot.com/2015/07/the-cimmerian-hypothesis-part-one.html

Niches are filled, the populations of wild animals shift and morph, and new plant species colonize, often to our chagrin. Nature grinds on, unconcerned with our desire to craft futures in our control and unconvinced by our claims of omnipotence.

This is perhaps the great flaw in our most common attempts to write about and predict the future. So many of the predictive stories we tell make humans dominant while attempting to bend the future to our will. They cleanse the future of its wildness. No matter how exciting or strange these stories portray their worlds, those elements most often stem from human constructs, control, beliefs, and ways of understanding the world. It is so rarely a strangeness created by the natural world because that's a strangeness we so often refuse to see or consider.

Here again is the challenge presented by this magazine and by the sub-genre of deindustrial science fiction. It calls us to set aside the overriding obsession within our culture for human-made futures and imagine the much stranger, more complex, and wild ones that actually are coming for us. The natural world—which we too often forget we're a part of, but which we do not control—will do far more to determine our future than we will, even if many of those future determinations are being driven by current human decisions. The future will be nature-made, not human-made, and while I suspect there are many aspects of it we aren't going to like, I also believe that it will surprise in a multitude of ways, and that a number of those surprises will prove wondrous. I believe there's a promise of unseen adventure in our future, just as I believe there's a promise of unfortunate and significant trouble.

Editing this magazine, I enjoy reading the ways in which different people see a future woven by nature, rather than humans. Too many stories still hit my inbox depicting futures crafted purely by humans. However, I am more and more receiving stories that depict futures of adaptation, in which humans cope with the realities brought to bear on them by forces far larger and more complex than we can ever begin to understand or mimic. These are the tales I find most fascinating. These are the tales I find delightful and joyous, sad and melancholy, painful and inspiring.

Ultimately, these are tales of human craft, but it's a human craft situated within the context and limits imposed by the natural world—not within a contextless human imagination untethered to the hard physical realities of our planet. It's these tales of human craft, constricted by the sort of realities we are likely to face, that I find most creative and inspiring. It's these sort of tales I want to publish. And it's these sort of tales you will find in the following pages.

Deindustrial science fiction is still in its early stages of development, but it holds great promise. I can't wait to see where it takes us. No doubt many stories, like nature, will surprise and delight, rising out of the darkness to help us see the world anew and to bring to mind unexpected and, with luck, better ways to live.

- Portland, Oregon
July 21, 2016

Into the Ruins is published quarterly by Figuration Press. We publish deindustrial science fiction that explores a future defined by natural limits, energy and resource depletion, industrial decline, climate change, and other consequences stemming from the reckless and shortsighted exploitation of our planet, as well as the ways that humans will adapt, survive, live, die, and thrive within this future.

One year, four issue subscriptions to *Into the Ruins* are $39. You can subscribe by visiting intotheruins.com or by mailing a check made out to Figuration Press to:

Figuration Press / 3515 SE Clinton Street / Portland, OR 97202

To submit your work for publication, please visit intotheruins.com/submissions or email submissions@intotheruins.com.

All issues of *Into the Ruins* are printed on paper, first and foremost. Electronic versions will be made available as high quality PDF downloads. Please visit our website for more information. The opinions expressed by the authors do not necessarily reflect the opinions of Figuration Press or *Into the Ruins*. Except those expressed by Joel Caris, since this is a sole proprietorship. That said, all opinions are subject to (and commonly do) change. The world, after all, is too confusing and complicated for opinions of it not to change. So finds the Editor.

──────── ADVERTISEMENT ────────

EDITOR-IN-CHIEF
JOEL CARIS

ASSOCIATE EDITOR
SHANE WILSON

DESIGNER
JOEL CARIS

WITH THANKS TO
SHANE WILSON
JOHN MICHAEL GREER
OUR SUBSCRIBERS

SPECIAL THANKS TO
KATE O'NEILL

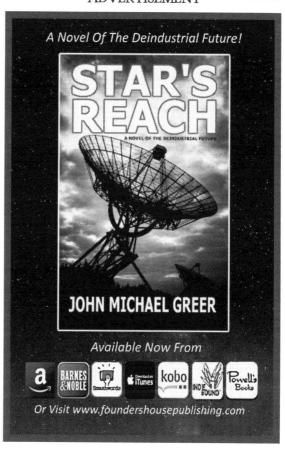

CONTRIBUTORS

W. JACK SAVAGE is a retired broadcaster and educator. He is the author of seven books, including *Imagination: The Art of W. Jack Savage* (wjacksavage.com). To date, more than fifty of Jack's short stories and over seven hundred of his paintings and drawings have been published worldwide. Jack and his wife Kathy live in Monrovia, California. Jack is again responsible for this issue's cover art.

CHLOE WOODS hails from the beautiful but damp city of Edinburgh, Scotland. She is about to start a Master's degree in Human Evolution and Behaviour, which combines her love of obscure topics that shouldn't be obscure and questions nobody can answer. She is also a trad fiddle player, a bird-watcher and an avid befriender of cats, and she has been working on the same piece of knitting for two years. Chloe is in her early twenties and she would like to be a writer when she grows up. This is her first formal publication.

BART HILLYER lives with his wife on a quiet street in Mascoutah, Illinois, about 30 miles from St. Louis. (His story "Red Wing" is situated in Mascoutah, circa 2120.) After retiring from 21 years of active duty Air Force service in 2004, the author has puttered and dabbled and muddled his way through several house rehab projects, including the 1906 Folk Victorian where he now lives. His current project is a 1963 Mid-Century Modern that's driving him crazy. Occasionally he writes a short story.

JOEL CARIS is a gardener and homesteader, occasional farmer, passionate advocate for local and community food systems, sporadic writer, voracious reader, sometimes prone to distraction and too attendant to detail, a little bit crazy, a cynical optimist, and both deeply empathetic toward and frustrated with humanity. He is your friendly local editor and publisher. As a reader of this and perhaps other editions of *Into the Ruins*, he hopes you don't too easily tire of his voice and perspective. He lives in Oregon with an amazing, endlessly patient woman who makes him shockingly happy.

G. KAY BISHOP is the type of writer who wants people to say App-ah-LATT-chi-an, not App-uh-LAY-shun. Plural vs. possessive apostrophes and post-prepositional pronouns properly placed in the objective case can also trigger avalanches of opinion. When in proximity, attach ears firmly to sides of head, tread softly, and carry a big shtick. Despite the danger, torrents of Bishop's opinions can be rewarding to observe from a safe distance. Collective housing, green-grocery, subscription libraries, and topographic maps are particularly sublime in season. Avoid psychosocial topics unless you are a trained professional.

Born in the gritty Navy town of Bremerton, Washington and raised in the south Seattle suburbs, **JOHN MICHAEL GREER** started writing about as soon as he could hold a pencil. He is the author of more than forty nonfiction books and four novels, including the deindustrial novel *Star's Reach*, as well as the weekly blog "The Archdruid Report," and has edited four volumes of the *After Oil* series of deindustrial SF anthologies. These days he lives in Cumberland, Maryland, an old red brick mill town in the north central Appalachians, with his wife Sara.

LAWRENCE BUENTELLO'S fiction has appeared in multiple publications and anthologies. He is the author of over ninety published short stories in a variety of genres. Buentello is also the author of the science fiction novel, *The Bridge of a Thousand Leagues*. He is a native of San Antonio, Texas.

JAY CUMMINGS lives and works on a small sustainable farm in Northwest Montana with his wife and three rambunctious little boys. In the summer, you'll find him prepping lettuce beds and tending to livestock. On long winter nights, you'll find him huddled in front of the wood stove working and reworking novels and novellas.

JUSTIN PATRICK MOORE, KE8COY, is a writer, radio hobbyist and student of the Mysteries. His work has been published in *Flurb*, *Witches and Pagans*, and *Abraxas: International Journal of Esoteric Studies*. His post-collapse novelette *Water In the Dry Land* is available free on his website sothismedias.com where he blogs about dreams, magic, art and culture in the age of industrial decline. Justin and his wife make their home in Cincinnati, the Queen of the West.

LETTERS TO THE EDITOR

Dear Editor,

I just finished reading every word of the first edition. I enjoyed all and can relate to some. Happy to say I am now a subscriber. It is very important to have stories. Stories define us now and shape our future.

As we lose the abundance we have enjoyed for several generations, will we see it coming? If not, we will look for a reason, blame others, and hunt for a scapegoat. It's the president, those damn foreigners, the atheists, or the Christians. Feel free to substitute any of a myriad of other choices.

The point is, a few have already accepted the fact that life is about to become much different. Some will no doubt get the message. Most I fear will fight to stay on the ship as it goes down, pulling others with them and causing grief in forms I hesitate to imagine.

Will we collectively recognize the economic, resource, and or energy contractions as they come and adjust accordingly? Or will we continue pushing the snowball we have created uphill until we can't, at which time it rolls back over us, flattening everything as it goes?

I fear the latter. We need a new story, or stories, before it's too late.

As the future unfolds, what will we lose, and what will we be able to hang on to? What might we gain?

We have so much better understanding of things like soil structure and organisms. Better tools, and even the so called heritage seeds are far more productive than one century ago. We now know that there is no need to plow up garden space. My parents and grandparents never saw a broadfork. Will we hang on to this knowledge? I have no idea.

The population issues will be corrected one way or another. The oceans, forest, and fields will recover and again be plentiful. It may take a very long time, but the earth is resilient. But will we have learned our lesson? Or will humans in some far distant time start the chaos all over again? Not if we have and keep our stories.

Thanks for a wonderful read, and a bit of hope. Anxiously awaiting the next issue.

Marty Pixley
Atlantic Beach, Florida

Dear Editor,

I want to bring to your attention a book that I think you and your readers would enjoy. I discovered the book *Inter States: Fossil Nation* by Ralph Meima through the Founders House Publishing website. They also publish some of John Michael Greer's titles.

The world that Ralph Meima

sketches falls in the middle of the future not ordered. The book follows a cast of characters as they deal with life in 2040s America. Characters are forced to deal with the consequences of peak-oil and climate change against the backdrop of reduced standards of living. In a future saturated with high technology, people struggle to find food, shelter and enough energy to heat their homes.

The value, for me, lies in the book's ability to show how believable characters deal with situations larger than themselves, while simultaneously dealing with the mundane realities of life on the downward slope of Hubbert's peak. It made me appreciate our current freedom of movement, privileges and energy abundance from the perspective of a future much poorer in these things.

The next book in the series, *Inter States: Emergent Disorder* was recently released and continues on from the cliffhanger ending of the first book.

I can highly recommend both books.

Regards,

Marcu Knoesen
Melbourne, Australia

Dear Editor,

I got talking with another Vietnam veteran at the gym today. You know, "Who were you with?" and so on. It got around to "A lot of guys are going back . . . how about you?" I'd love to see Vietnam again . . . in piece because it's so beautiful there. I have no doubt at all I'd love it. But I'm slowing down to the point where I sold my mountain bike last week because I know my next fall would probably land me in the hospital. In the same way, and I know it sounds crazy, but I'm too old to run away from death anymore. So I have this dream where this guy goes into this bar where death is having a few cocktails and says, "Oh yeah, and that guy Savage from the 1st Cav, just got off the plane in Saigon. Says he's heading up the coast." A slow smile curls Death's lips and after taking a sip of his drink says . . . "Yeah. . . . Savage . . . I remember him. Where's he staying? Maybe I should go and say hello." The truth is, I should have died in Vietnam nearly fifty years ago . . . more than once. I have tried to become more, do more, and live a life some of the guys who didn't make it would have been at least proud to have lived, had they had the chance. This kind of thinking made alcoholics of more than a few of us who survived and I knew long ago all I could do was live my life beyond anything they might have achieved. But going back to Vietnam would seem to me like whistling in the graveyard. I took a very laissez faire attitude toward my life after Vietnam. And now all of a sudden, I jealously want to extend every minute I have left. These are Memorial Day thoughts, of course. When we were in the 8th Field Hospital in Nha Trang, my buddy Rick

Gillum and I talked about these things. He was dead a month later and now it's fifty or more years after that and I'm holding on to all that he never got to experience. So, I am of two minds . . . make time to go there and the hell with it, or sit around doing what I do . . . like being on goal when playing tag as a kid where you can't be tagged "It" anymore.

Take care,

Jack Savage, Cover Artist
Monrovia, California

Dear Editor,

I do not know if this topic fits within the structure of your "Letters to the Editor" section, but I'd like to offer up a recent experience of mine for consideration.

To give a name to the thing, I would suggest something along the lines of "Class, Status, and the Grand Illusion"—perhaps a stodgy, academic-sounding title, but descriptive of my experience. Just recently, I returned to my Wisconsin home from a trip to parts further south, an annual visit with family. My parents, now retired, have settled in an upscale community in northern Florida. During my week-long visit, I had a subroutine running in the back of my mind, observing the aspects of class and status in their community (the house models, amenities, general lifestyle and the nature of retail in the vicinity). Now, my parents have certainly done well

and retired much more comfortably and at a higher level than we lived for much of my childhood (we were solidly middle class, rising from the lower end of that band to the higher end over the years). My father in fact commented on his surprise that he and my mother had managed to retire in this style as financially feasibly as they have.

Being in this kind of environment has an impact on you. During the course of the trip, moving through the airports both going and returning, observing the lifestyles and amenities in this community, I found myself desiring the kind of status and wealth that would enable such living—the home office, the home suitable for social entertaining, corporate prestige, and what have you. Simultaneously, I wrestled with a sense of guilt, knowing that these lifestyles are not only unsustainable, but given limited resources, also further deplete the resource bank upon which the rest of society depends. This internal conflict slowly grew in intensity, peaking on the return journey during the two legs of our flight.

Then, as we drove the final stretch homeward, north out of Milwaukee, through the farmland of Ozaukee, Sheboygan, and Manitowoc counties, through the small towns and villages that dot the landscape, I felt the conflict dissipate as the craving and desire slipped away—the illusion of wealth and status I had witnessed faded in the light of the wealth of the land and the power of enough. It was a fascinating internal experience to witness, as I was fully aware of what was occurring even as it happened.

My take-away, for what it is worth, is that the grand illusion is very powerful. It will overwhelm your perspective, even when you are presented with only a modest version of it (I was in an upscale community, but by no means an upper 1% community). But when you step away from that environment, that power can and does fade. Maintaining the necessary awareness of these processes is key to distinguishing between illusion and reality.

David England
Two Rivers, Wisconsin

Into the Ruins *welcomes letters to the editor from our readers. We encourage thoughtful commentary on the contents of this issue, the themes of the magazine, and humanity's collective future, as well as recommendations of other works of deindustrial science fiction. Readers may email their letters to editor@intotheruins.com, or send by mail to:*

Figuration Press
3515 SE Clinton Street
Portland, OR 97202

Further information available at:
intotheruins.com/letters

Author's and editor's notes of erratum for "Coyote Year," published Spring 2016, Issue #1:

Dear Readers,

For "sextant," please read "chronometer." No blame to our excellent editor; I believe I sent him the earlier version instead of my more recent one. Due to text conversion issues and carelessness on my part, the matter escaped me. Apologies to those seafaring folk who know that a sextant is less costly to make than a sea-worthy timepiece.

G.Kay Bishop, Author

Dear Readers,

In publication of G.Kay Bishop's fine and adventurous story, "Coyote Year," I failed to include below the story's title the labeling of said story as "A Many Nations Tale," despite inclusion of this information by the author. While she has been generous enough to lay no blame on me for the above-noted sextant/chronometer error, the blame for lack of proper labeling of "Coyote Year" lies fully upon myself.

Please note that Bishop's excellent and also-adventurous story, "Spyne Drift," which is included in this issue, is a Many Nations tale, as well. This time, you shall find it so labeled.

Apologies to both our contributing author and our readers.

Joel Caris, Editor

STORIES

Time's Ark
by Jay Cummings

Azra moved slowly and deliberately to the stately display table where
three seemingly unrelated objects rested next to one another with ceremonial intention. The room, its slowfan turning listlessly above smooth, time-polished
wooden desks, began to fill with a wide variety of people representing great diversity. This gathering was unique. Invited were top scholars from most circles, but
also students and apprentices, some quite young. Mixed in were members of the
trades—mostly builders and inventors. A few continuity elders edged their way into the back rows. Azra's own most senior apprentice, Kori, sat quietly to the side of
an imposing lectern, in front of a covered easel.

The chatter and greetings of fellows too long separated, now well met, died
down after a time. People took seats and found comfortable spots to stand around
the back wall. Attention turned to the front of the room. Azra never used the
lectern, it's sides polished and worn from generations of nervous hands grasping for
safety. Instead, he forced himself out in front of it, to stand in full view of his audience. Even after all these years, this was an effort. He much preferred the cordiality
and cooperation of a small group. Yet, he knew this type of presentation was an important tool that he must use, however uncomfortable he might be.

Without thinking, he picked up the potted plant. "Welcome," he began, and
waited respectfully for the echoed welcoming response from his audience. There, in
the back, he caught a glimpse of Shakre. *Good. She's come. The real meeting will be
later with her and* . . . He didn't know how to finish that thought.

"Thank you for coming," he continued. "You will no doubt be wondering why
I have invited such a . . . hmm . . . *diverse* mix of people to come listen to an old man
teach." Azra accepted a small wave of lighthearted laughter. His audience knew
without questioning that if he called a meeting for a lesson, anyone invited would

stop what they were doing and make the journey.

"I haven't taught a lesson in quite some time. My apprentices and contemporaries are quite capable of carrying on the Subjects." He paused and glanced at Kori, who smiled back at him. "They are really quite remarkable, these fellows I have had the privilege to work with these long years. Our future seems to be in good hands.

"But I am not here to speak of the future, fascinating and beguiling though the future may be." He set the potted plant down, and picked up the folded piece of parchment that lay next to it. "I am here to speak on the subject of the past." He opened the letter and scanned it for a moment. "This, you may know, is a seed letter. You have all written them, and you know them to be an important part of our continuity." In the back of the crowd, one or two of the continuity elders nodded in assent.

"This happens to be my letter." Azra smiled wide and the crowd laughed with him. "My letter, like yours, I suspect, shows me . . . no, demonstrates to me the need for continuity elders and their wisdom. Among other dangers and pitfalls, without this wisdom, we are likely to mistake the hasty truths of youth for the guiding and eternal truths of Natural Law." He paused. "Embarrassing though they may be." Again, the crowd broke into a respectful laughter.

"But I'm not here to lecture on continuity either. Rather, I'd like for you to look at this seed letter as a metaphor. We write them when we are young. The continuity elders keep them safe until we have reached an age where we have power and capability, but need the wisdom of perspective in order to use that capability to bring the Web a vigorous and healthy today, and an excellent foundation for tomorrow, within the bounds of Natural Law.

"They are, in a sense, an ark that travels along the river of time. What is necessary for them to successfully navigate that river is a safe haven from the ravages of this river: time. Surely, some letters are lost to accident or some such, but as a small but important part of their work, the elders do a generally good job of providing these arks with the means to get from one moment in time, to a much later moment in time."

Azra could sense the continuity elders hovering somewhere between pleased and cautious. From their perspective, Azra's profession was a necessary evil. He didn't think a little flattery would hurt, but he was under no illusions that it would help them accept his work with any kind of charity or support.

"Now imagine—could we write a seed letter to our children? Actually, I know some that do. It's not the prerogative of the elders to facilitate this sort of communication, but I'm sure they'd approve. I myself, as a young man, wrote a seed letter to my grandchildren. I think that was before I was handfasted, even. Now that's confidence." He smiled and again the audience greeted him with a respectful, quiet laughter.

"What if you wanted to write a seed letter to your great-great grandchildren? Now you start running into practical difficulties. Who will keep this letter? For surely, you will perish before it's intended recipients are even born. And what will you write it on? Our best parchment, kept dry and safe from accident or even sunlight, might last this long. Now what if you wished to send a seed letter to your great-great-great-great-great grandchildren?" Azra paused and spread his hands wide, inviting comment.

A young man in the front raised his hand, palm open. Azra nodded to him. He rose and spoke with surprising confidence to the group. "I am Jaqar, a seventh student in this, the Central circle." Azra nodded again for him to continue. "Perhaps, teacher, a person might carve a stone into a statue, with a message—written or pictorial."

"Yes," said Azra, simply—without the exaggerated praise in his voice another teacher might reserve for so young a student. "This is so. We have many such objects, and we make many such objects. As you all know, the Central Stone is fifteen generations old, and while we have made many conventions and refinements to our way of living, the basic tenants that protect and guide us are written there. And we hope that this stone will still be right where it is now for fifteen more generations, and fifteen after that.

"But we know from the work of our continuity elders, that time does not allow for stillness. It is Natural Law—all things are born, they live, then they die. That this is true for me, means it is true for you. It is true for all things. Even stones." There was more nodding from the elders in the back, but one elder in particular was scowling. Azra smiled in his direction.

"But because we have these two examples, the paper and the stone, we can see that different things succumb to the ravages of time at different rates. Indeed, the artifacts we still sometimes discover from the world before are a testament to the longevity of some materials resting in particular environments.

"I will simplify, and propose the following: If you wish to maximize the longevity of an object, then make it from materials of extremely high durability, like a very durable stone, or the metals of antiquity, and place it in a highly stable, secure environment—somewhere dry where thieves would not plunder." Again Azra opened his hands palm out, but he didn't really expect anyone to disagree. These were, he thought, facts even young school children could grasp.

"Now," he said. At this, the audience leaned in just a little. "We know the Ancients were powerful—very powerful, but also careless. We have few messages from them, and really our only evidence that they walked the earth at all is the very fact of the longevity of some of the materials they created. Our brightest minds and most skilled metallurgists cannot replicate many of the materials they have left us. Our very best estimates are that the Ancients passed from this world more than fifty generations ago." Azra stopped to let this sink in. These figures were not a secret, but neither were they settled. Many scholars would not accept that a culture could have existed so long ago that was as powerful as the few objects they left behind suggested. Nevertheless, Azra pushed on.

"I said a moment ago, the Ancients were careless. We assume they must have been. How could a civilization with so much power and so much knowledge allow itself to burn brightly and then fade, as we see the barbarians beyond our most distant walls do so very often?" Azra looked around the room, but did not signal for commentary, instead leaving his question to hang in the air. He carefully set the letter down and picked up the hammer that lay on the table next to it.

"This hammer was my father's hammer. He was a builder, a great one. Many of our best structures in Central circle have his sweat and love in them. He gave this hammer to me when I came to fifth year. It could be that, deep down, he wished I would have become a builder as well—this despite what we know to be true of Natural Law, that each person is charged with forging their own path." Azra stopped to remember the man for just a moment, bringing the truth of feeling to his speech. "I believe he loved me unconditionally. Still, good men make mistakes. Like my father, we are human, and make human errors—each according to their peculiar flaws. Therefore, if we can say anything about humans as a group, it is that while we share similarities, we are all very different from one another, capable of great kindness, great sorrow, and all things between. Can it be that every Ancient was uniformly careless? By this logic, that must be impossible. What if there were some who saw the error that ended their power?" Azra set down the hammer, but did not invite comment.

"Imagine a boat which springs a leak. You start to bail the water out, but you see that this is futile. Around you is only open ocean, and it is clear that if you bail water, you might slow the descent of your craft, but you see that it will eventually fail no matter what you do. There is no land near enough to swim to, and no other boats on the water. Your fate is to drown. How will you spend your last moments? Will you bail water hopelessly? Will you meditate in prayer to prepare yourself for what comes after we die?

"Surely there were Ancients who saw the end coming and tried each of these. But there is one small possibility that I would like to discuss. If you had a pen, some paper, and a bottle, you might write a note, say something true about your life. You might write a story or a poem, an explanation, or an apology, something to communicate with the future, your predicament, your hopes, your fears. Something meaningful to pass along. You might write that note, pop it into the bottle, and throw it over the side as your ship slipped below the waves and you breathed your last few breaths in this life." Azra mimed putting a cork into a bottle and tossing it to those students in the first rows before him.

"If you were an Ancient, and you could see the end of your civilization coming, would you reach for that pen? Maybe just one or two might. But you might also grasp the length of night coming upon the world. What material would you use? Where would you put that message? What could possibly expect to survive fifty or more generations?" Azra opened his palms wide, suggesting a broad call for input.

A tall, middle-aged woman stood. "I am Rakell, from Third circle east over the mountains. I am a scholar of three degrees. I would put my message, whatever the material, in strong desert rock. Perhaps the red rocks of the Nikal deserts." Azra nodded, but said nothing. Another young man stood. "I am Tokal from the Second circle west of the Singing lakes. I am a master in the building trades. I would build a great ark for my message to sit within, to protect it from time and thievery." Again Azra nodded but didn't say anything. At last a continuity elder raised his hand. Azra was surprised; they usually spoke very little. He stood. "I am Jindall. I am a Third level continuity elder in this Central circle. I would make it from as large a block of the metal that does not rust as I possibly could."

"All good arguments," said Azra. "Each with a weakness. Deserts shift and change. What was once desert might, in the course of two hundred and fifty generations, become a lake bed or river way. Great arks are no less subject to the vagaries of time than the objects that reside within, and would so perish over time. A great mass of the metal which does not rust would be a very tempting target for looters and thieves."

The audience fell silent. Azra again picked up the potted plant. "This," he said slowly, "is an Althea plant. It's a shrub, actually. It thrives in dry, desert environments. Its life cycle is very interesting. Can anyone tell us how it reproduces?" He paused. "No? Hmm, I'll have to have a talk with our botany scholars . . ." This time, no one laughed at his joke.

"In the desert from which this plant comes, rain sometimes doesn't come at all. For years at a time. In order to survive and reproduce, when it does rain, this shrub very quickly creates tiny spores. They look like seeds, and there are seeds inside. But what we see when we look at the spores are actually very resilient shells. The seeds inside may lay dormant for years, even generations. When just the right conditions reappear, the spore opens, and the plant seed takes root.

Azra looked around the room at the many silent faces. "Before I go on, I would ask that you ponder the following question: If the Ancients were able to leave us a seed letter or an ark of sorts, what would be in it?" He stood silently, watching students and masters alike shift nervously for a moment. "What would they say to us?"

Finally, into the silence that followed, Azra spoke. "I have brought these three items here to demonstrate the vastly different possibilities. The letter, a symbol of wisdom and advice. The hammer, a symbol of hopes and dreams for the future. The plant, a symbol of passing on heritage—a way of perpetuating a culture. There are doubtless other possibilities, and I grant"—he paused, looking several of his audience members directly in the eye—"I grant that this conversation might be better presented as a thought experiment on a cold day over a warm cup of tea. Except." He motioned to his most senior apprentice. She stood and went to an easel covered in cloth behind the lectern, bringing it out and uncovering it. "Except, that we have found just such an ark."

Azra stood silently while his audience broke out into a disbelieving cacophony. When finally his audience took control of themselves and returned to the restraint accorded a lesson brought by a teacher of Azra's status, he spoke again, this time more rapidly and with a practiced brevity. "Many of you will know of my teacher's teacher, Argus. His life's work was to build on his teacher's work involving the force that binds us to the Earth. Argus was very skilled in the language of math, and made a great many discoveries. He added a great deal to our knowledge of Natural Law.

"When you jump off of a cliff, for instance, Natural Law dictates that you must fall to the ground. Argus and his apprentices put numbers and order to this Law. We now understand it very well. My mentor, Sanis, followed his work and described many useful applications of this Law. My own work, for many many years, followed along these lines.

"However, I have a somewhat broader calling. I am very interested in continuity, especially in the paths taken by those who've come before. It was perhaps ten years ago that I came across the work of Calthus, a scholar who lived roughly six generations ago. Calthus taught in an unusual way. Scholars today mainly take an idea, or a set of ideas, and explore them. Calthus did this, but he added a very important nuance to his work. Whatever question or idea was before him, he always asked of it, 'What are the natural consequences of this idea?' Now this may not seem strange or unusual, but really it is. It's one thing to work out a formula that describes an observation. It's quite another to see the far-reaching consequences of knowing this formula. I began to try to ask this question of my work.

"Remember, my work regards the force that holds us to the Earth. I began to throw balls into the air. With more force, I could throw them very far before they'd fall back to the Earth. Extending this simple action to it's logical, yet counter-intuitive conclusion, could there be an object which was traveling so fast, thrown with such force, that it might fall forever, and never come back to the Earth? The amount of force that seemed necessary was ridiculous. But it is not ridiculous if you are far enough away. Indeed, we have shown that the moon slips around the Earth according to these same Laws that govern the force that holds us to the Earth. It is, in effect, falling forever and ever."

Azra stopped for a moment to let this all sink in. Very few of the people in the audience would have had the training to pick apart his assertions with any veracity. Not one face, however, showed confusion or betrayed ignorance. He continued. "If one thinks carefully enough about this fact, and the natural consequences of this fact, there is a rather unusual truth that must emerge. If an object is close to the Earth, it will rub against the air, and come under the influence of the force that holds us to the Earth, and fall from the sky. By the Laws worked out so many years ago, it is clear also that if an object is too far from the Earth, forces other than those which hold us to the Earth will capture it and it will fly away into the heavens. Because we know that Natural Law holds true for both these conditions, a third condition must exist. A condition where an object is neither so close that it falls to Earth, nor too far that it flies away: a condition of equilibrium would exist, where an object would be frozen in one spot in the heavens—doomed to circle the Earth forever. The moon is such an object, though it is quite possible, even probable, that it is either falling very slowly to the Earth, or flying slowly away."

Azra stepped next to the easel, which featured Kori's drawing of the object. It was long and rectangular with several squares budding from each side. Even without much detail, the object was clearly artificial. "And so, if you were an Ancient, and you wanted to preserve something for a very very long time, and if you had the means to do it, would you not put your ark into one of these locations?" Azra smiled as a few heads nodded in the audience. "Safe from looters and wind and weather. Why, you'd even guarantee that whoever found your ark was sufficiently advanced to appreciate whatever it might contain, or, of considerably greater potential, what might be written upon it, given how difficult a task it would be to even find it in the sky.

"We have glimpsed it several times using our newest and most powerful instruments, and while we cannot see it with exceptional clarity—yet—many eyes have verified the form that Kori has put on paper. You can see it is quite man-made." Many in the audience leaned very far forward in their desks to get a glimpse of the angular image. It would have been exceptionally rude to get up out of their desks during the lesson, but it was clear many wanted to.

"If our math is right, there will be an opportunity to view this object tonight, as long as the weather stays clear. We have set up our instruments, and will invite three or four of our most senior guests today to see for themselves." Azra smiled, but his insides were in knots. He knew that one of the guests of honor at the observatory would be the senior continuity elder in the back who was not murmuring amongst his neighbors as his colleagues seemed to be, but rather was staring directly at Azra with a decidedly unpleasant frown.

‡‡

"You're mad," Shakre said, putting away her third mug of bitters. "You know the elders will tear this apart. Hell, half the scholars think you should be forced into retirement."

"And the other half?" Azra asked, drinking his tea.

"Well," Shakre smiled, "the other half want to bestow upon you an unprecedented seventh degree."

Azra snorted. "It's all foolishness. This discovery will change nothing. We certainly don't have the means to get to the ark, though I suppose we can build more powerful equipment with which to view it. It's interesting, but I fear it is nothing more than a tantalizing dead end."

"That's not how the continuity elders will see it."

"You're right about that. Many will see this discovery like they see everything we do, as a threat. But again, to what end? All there will be is talk." Azra drained his tea and motioned to the barkeep for another.

Shakre looked at him. A smile spread across her face. "You don't believe a word of that, do you?"

Azra feigned disbelief. "I don't know what you're talking about."

"You were the one who called us all here. You called young boys and old men. You called builders and elders among scholars. You made sure every person in every circle would know as immediately as possible about this discovery. What this lesson really was, was you lighting a fire."

"A fire?"

"Yes," continued Shakre. "You want others to pick up this discovery like a torch, and carry it on. To pick up your work. You're looking to pass this discovery on to, well, to whoever is excited by it."

"And is that a crime?" Azra turned serious. "All we have left of the Ancients are fragments, little bits and pieces that tell us of their awesome power, but tell us nothing of them, and who they were. Now we have this. An ark. A complete . . . well, it's a complete work of theirs. A whole thing. Surely it's there to survive the ages. Surely it's there to be that message in the bottle. We must pluck that message out. We must know what became of them. We must know of their glory. We must know of the fire that burned so bright in their culture that it burned them to ashes."

"But"—Shakre used a gentle tone now—"why?"

"Because," said Azra. He paused for a very long time, looking into a distance Shakre couldn't see. "Our fate, despite what the continuity elders would have us believe, is to become the Ancients."

For once, Shakre didn't know what to say. What Azra had just said was completely original and extremely forbidden. She had never put thoughts together in this way, and yet she knew, without hesitation, that what Azra suggested was blasphemy. If the continuity elders heard him speak in this way, he would be put on trial, and exiled at the very least. The two old friends looked at each other, and for the first time in their long lives as colleagues and friends, Shakre felt that she didn't know the man sitting in the next chair. She did not know him at all.

At the funeral, Jaqar sat quietly with his mother and tried to match her stoicism. Despite his best efforts, he could not withhold his tears as many of the Web's finest artisans and musicians paid tribute to who was arguably the greatest, if not the most controversial, scholar any generation had known. He felt anxious beneath his grief.

Five years had passed since the day he sat in the main lecture hall of the largest scholarly campus in all of the Web. Three days after Azra's famous lecture on the ancient Ark, Jaqar had approached him. As a seventh year, it was his responsibility to determine the direction his studies would take him. Just one year after shedding his childhood, Jaqar was a strong and advanced student. This fact was why he had been invited to the lecture in the first place. On that day, Jaqar had known with certainty that to study and understand the Ark was his destiny.

When he had shed his childhood, he wrote the customary seed letter. But upon seeing the Ark, Jaqar knew he needed to write another. So he lay in wait. He knew that Azra often took tea in the afternoon at the campus canteen, and would cross the main quad from his working quarters and laboratories to get there. He stationed himself on a likely looking bench near the path he believed the famous scholar would take.

"Excuse me, sir," he had said. Jaqar had always had a deep reserve of confidence. Still, his stomach filled with a most unpleasant churning.

"Why yes, young lad," Azra said kindly, with a smile. "You are Jaqar, are you not? A seventh?"

Jaqar was taken aback. Certainly someone as important as this man would not know of a mere seventh student? But again, Jaqar brought up his nerve and smiled back. "Yes, sir," he said, hoping his voice did not betray the ebullience threatening to overtake his faculties.

"What can I do for you? I'm just on my way for tea—will you walk with me?"

Jaqar quickly fell in beside Azra, and they began walking together. "Sir, if I might, I have a question about your lesson the other day."

"Just one?" Azra laughed.

Jaqar realized that Azra was playing with him, and he relaxed a little. "Well, of course there are many questions and few answers, I suspect, but I have a question I think you can help me with."

"Go ahead, young man," Azra said.

"Well," began Jaqar, "I shed my childhood around a year ago, and so I've already written my seed letter, but I'd like to write myself another."

Azra smiled a little, and then abruptly stopped himself. "I see," he said neutrally.

"Yes." They were approaching the canteen now, and Jaqar's words started to tumble out. "I want to figure a way to send myself this seed letter without the help of the continuity elders, and I was wondering—you said in your lesson that you sent one to your grandchildren. I was wondering how you did that?"

Azra stopped, and so Jaqar stopped. The elder scholar turned and looked into Jaqar's face, searching his youthful features. "And just why do you want to send a seed letter to yourself now?"

Jaqar wasn't prepared for this question. He thought Azra might brush his question aside with a platitude, or even offer some small advice. The answer, though, was clear as day to Jaqar. "I'd like to remind my older self—an older self who will probably be exhausted and facing many dead-ends, and who knows what kinds of obstacles—just how excited I feel right now."

Azra didn't say anything. His silence made Jaqar nervous. *What if he thinks me a fool?* But it was too late. It was too late to go back now. So he said, "You see, I'd like to study the Ark, and . . . and I have the feeling that this course of study will have, well, many difficulties." He hesitated, then added quickly, "And I want to help myself through those times by preserving in a letter just how excited I am right now."

Azra remained quiet a long time. He took a deep breath, looked up into the sky, then back down into the face of this youth and said, "If this is so, come to my study tomorrow at midday, and I will help you craft the letter you describe. You are wise to anticipate adversity, but I fear you don't know even the half of it."

This was the beginning of Jaqar's work on the Ark. He followed normal courses as any student in the maths would do, but then once each week he would meet with Azra. Sometimes they discussed the physical shape of the Ark and what the various geometric protrusions might be for, what they might mean, and most importantly, what might be written there. Azra began to teach him the math that predicted the Ark's place in the sky.

After several months, Azra took him to the observatory one clear night and showed Jaqar the Ark. This was a transformational experience for the young man. Knowing that such a rare and special thing existed was enough for Jaqar, but actually seeing it solidified in his heart the need to understand and study this object. Experiencing the physicality of it deeply moved him.

Jaqar didn't pay much attention to the world outside of the scholar's campus, but one day, when Jaqar showed up at Azra's door, he found the old scholar getting his coat and scarf on. They headed out on a walk. This wasn't their usual routine, but Jaqar found that Azra enjoyed surprising his young charge. He explained, "Good habits make for good work, but breaking good habits is necessary for making great work."

They walked away from campus and past the student residences. They took small paths until they were at the main square. On one end of the main square stood the House of Laws. Azra boldly walked with Jaqar up to the main entrance of this imposing structure. Made of crimson-fired bricks, three stories tall, it stood as high as any building in the Web. Jaqar had never been inside. A sentry at the door asked about their business, and while Azra said something vague and non-committal about teaching, the sentry, like everyone in all the Web, knew who Azra was, and wasn't about to deny him entry.

They walked up a series of stairs and down a hallway until they came to a set of doors. Azra opened them, and motioned for Jaqar to enter. Jaqar found himself on a balcony, overlooking a large chamber filled with desks and several men and women milling about.

"The Great Sieve," Jaqar said.

"Yes," replied his mentor. "This is the place where every major decision in the Web is put to the test of whether or not it follows what we know to be Natural Law."

They stood and watched the people below for a time, and then Jaqar asked, "Teacher, why are we here?"

Azra turned to face his student. "Because someday, you will have to come here. You will have to face those people you see below. You will have to bring your very best arguments and insights. You must be convincing and thorough."

Jaqar wanted to hide his confusion but he knew better than to do that with Azra. "But why? What will I be arguing for? Or against?"

Azra held his hands open in a gesture inviting Jaqar to answer his own question.

Jaqar turned and looked back at the people in the chamber below. They looked so serious. "It must have to do with the Ark." Still Azra invited him to finish his own line of reasoning. "What about studying the Ark has to do with questions of Natural Law?"

"Ah," Said Azra at last. "This is the right question. Now answer it."

Jaqar thought hard. His own experience with the Ark had been nothing but exciting, but he did know that some people felt differently. "Some people don't like that the Ark is such a direct connection to the Ancients?"

"Yes," said Azra as he put his hand on Jaqar's shoulder, a rare moment of affection that Jaqar found embarrassing, but also endearing. "Yes," Azra repeated.

That day seemed a very long time ago now as mourners lined up to pay their last respects. Jaqar joined the line, while his mother stayed in her seat. When it was his turn, Jaqar went up to Azra's motionless body and put his hand on his mentor's shoulder in the same affectionate manner that his teacher had those years ago.

All at once, Jaqar realized that Azra had been a shield for himself and the other students working on the Ark. Now that shield was gone, and they'd have to find their own way forward with their studies. Jaqar looked hard into the face of his mentor. Just three days before they'd had tea together in the afternoon as they often did. Today, he was gone. His face still and emotionless, his hands clasped respectfully. There was nothing here of the lively and warm man he had been. He didn't want to leave his friend and teacher, though finally he moved past, and back to the seats where his mother waited.

She put a hand over his and said, "It will be okay, Jaqar."

"Will it?" he replied uncertainly.

"Of course it will. You will make it okay." She gave his hand a squeeze. "You will make it okay."

Jaqar stood silently among the ashes and rubble of the new observatory. Puffs of steam jagged up into the morning sunshine. His most senior apprentice, Delia, stood next to him. She took his hand. "Jaqar," she said. Everything was quiet around them now. The tumultuous previous days were over. There was nothing left to save now.

"Jaqar," she said again. He turned to her and gently took his hand from hers. She imagined, behind his face, a raging anger or depthless sadness. Perhaps some of both. But his face showed only wistful peace.

"My mother said to me once, when I was a very young man, when I had suffered a very great loss, she said to me, 'It will be okay Jaqar, you will make it so.' I believed her, and in fact it was. The next years were exciting years, and we made so many advances. Every season a new, more detailed drawing. We even forged allies in the House of Laws. So many exciting years. But we didn't see it. We didn't see how dark fear can be, how—" he paused as he came to the large, crumpled mass in the center of the ruins. He reached down with a gloved hand, picking through the wreckage. Finally, he stood, holding a small chunk of amorphous glass, frosted with smoke and coated in grime. "Think what we might have seen with this, Delia. Think."

"I . . . I'm so sorry Jaqar." Delia wished she had more comforting words. "This was your life's work, and—"

Jaqar cut her off. "No, Delia. This is not my life's work." Turning the piece of glass over in his hand, he found an unmarred surface and held it to the sun. "My life's work is just about to begin."

It took Delia a moment to take this in. "What do you mean?"

"Think of my mentor, Delia."

"The great Azra, of course."

"Now," said Jaqar, "what was his life's work?"

She looked at him quizzically. He rarely asked simple questions. In fact, Jaqar rarely asked questions of Delia at all. He preferred to let her discover important questions on her own. They had worked together so closely, for so many years that they had long ago dispensed with the standard teacher-apprentice formalities. Yet, he stood with his hands spread wide, inviting—no, demanding—a response. She answered slowly. "He . . . worked on the force that binds us to the earth. This helped him predict the existence of the Ark. Finding the Ark was his life's work."

Jaqar smiled. "No, Delia. It was not." He turned to the sun and closed his eyes for a minute, feeling its warmth. "No," he said finally, "*I* was his life's work."

"Wait. What do you mean?"

"I was his life's work, Delia. Myself and the others. You. It came to me in the night last night, in a moment of profound despair: His life's work wasn't just finding the Ark. His life's work was attracting young scholars who would be excited by the Ark and its possibilities. His life's work was transforming the Ark from a curiosity to a calling. We built this incredible observatory. Think what it might have seen! Not just the Ark, but the planets—distant stars. Johanas is working out a method for determining how distant a star is in the sky! Imagine if he could have used this observatory. Just imagine." Jaqar smiled at her again.

Delia could sense where he was going, but she pressed him to finish his thought. "But what is there to smile about, Jaqar? Now those things will not come to pass. Now all is ruined. Do you think the House of Laws will permit the offsets to build yet another observatory? The elders will go crazy."

Jaqar's smile turned wry. "Yes, the elders. You and I both know it was the elders who started this fire."

"Jaqar, we don't know that." She said.

"Of course we do," he said with a casual kindness. He was never one to be abrupt when in disagreement.

"Even so, what hope is there? Think of the years of effort just that one sliver of glass cost. Think of the expertise put into it that wasn't directed somewhere else. It's"—she paused, searching for the right words—"unovercomeable."

Jaqar laughed. "I love it when you come up with such terms! 'Unovercomeable,' indeed." He laughed again. "You're right, of course. The elders and their allies in the House will block any attempt to rebuild. Of course they know they will succeed. Building the observatory was assented to by only the slimmest of margins. Much was sacrificed. Anyone with eyes will see that." He turned back to the sun once again. "But think again on Azra. His life's work wasn't discovering the Ark. It was forging a path toward finding a way to study it, to make it a part of our lives and our culture and our stories. He passed on the will and excitement to carry the study forward, into the future." He stopped to inhale deeply. "My work, Delia—my life's work—will be to do the same. Only at this point"—he kicked at some of the still smoldering ashes—"we must look beyond filling the next generation with wonder about something exciting in the sky. We must forge a path here on the ground. We must forge a path to a place where this can never happen again."

‡‡

A more exciting night had never passed. The great room where Richa and her fellows gathered was abuzz, everyone talking to everyone.

"It's happened, it's happened!"

"The second circle west of the Singing lakes has fallen, it's ours!"

"Azra lives tonight!"

"The fifth circle on the Southern border has fallen to us!"

Richa and her friends cheered as each new message came gurgling over the wire. "The Plan," as it was simply known to her and her colleagues, was unfolding now. In this circle, the seventh circle in the Northern plains, there was very little support for the elders. What few supporters remained were escorted, without violence, to the edge of the circle, and asked not to return. They didn't ask nicely, but nobody got hurt.

Suddenly, Richa's friend Ace, who was manning the telegraph machine, fell silent. His shift in mood caught everyone's attention and the room grew silent. Then he spoke with a catch in his voice. "In the . . . the fifth circle East of the great forest, there was violence. Many were killed. The circle burns."

Silence echoed after this last statement. They all knew that the elders would not go quietly, but their plan had been so carefully crafted to avoid major conflict. The Arkers, as they called themselves, carefully chose circles to turn quite long ago, and then, while Jaqar was making the expected pleas for support at the Great Sieve in the Central circle, the Arkers quietly developed on-the-ground support in strategically chosen circles. Jaqar had known the elders would try to attempt a coup at the House of Laws and would likely succeed. Each Arker sympathizer in the House had long ago devised an escape plan to leave the Central circle. Quietly, and carefully, Arker sympathizers had shifted to their chosen circles in the weeks before. Jaqar himself stayed behind to continue to bang on the drums to keep up the appearance the Arkers were simply trying to win support in the House of Laws as they had always done.

Maybe they had been too bold in making their escape. "The Plan" allowed for the elders to take control of the Central circle. But the strategically chosen circles the Arkers did attempt to wrest control of were easily defensible, connected together and to resources, and most importantly, would divide the remaining territories controlled by the elders in half. They didn't have to win in each circle. They would simply cut off the elders' access to resources. Over time, the remaining circles would come to their side either by choice, or because they would realize they couldn't continue on, separated and isolated.

Maybe the elders sensed "The Plan." Jaqar had been a loud distraction in the House of Laws and no one knew if he had planned for escape or not, but perhaps the elders could feel the mechinations under the surface. Whatever the case, in the fifth circle East of the great forest, they did not go peacefully. There were now more reports of fighting and looting. Then a message calling for help. Then silence.

Richa and her friends echoed that silence.

Then another circle met the same fate. A small circle close to the ocean—sixth East of the sea—fell to violence and chaos. Reports of successful takeovers continued, but did not carry the joy that the news had brought earlier in the evening. Richa and her friends stayed up late into the evening until finally the sun returned in the east. Each circle in "The Plan" had reported now. Twelve successful takeovers. Three burned to the ground.

"What should we do?" asked someone.

"What *can* we do?" asked another.

Richa knew. She'd actually worked with Jaqar, anticipating this very day.

"We must secure the government and security forces of this circle," she said loudly. "Then we must go to the other circles where there has been violence, and find out what has come to pass." She paused. "And offer what assistance we can."

Richa's back ached. She pulled the crank back on her crossbow again, loaded her missile, took aim, and let a bolt fly loose. She automatically reached for the crank to load another while she watched her charge arc up, then fall silently into the lines of barricades before her. She didn't actually expect to hit anyone. Her small group was laying down a covering fire to keep the forces loyal to the elders from advancing.

Actually, they were trying to keep those forces occupied while a larger group attempted to flank them. She didn't know much about the larger battle plan in this circle. She didn't much care. She was weary from days that had turned into weeks and now months of conflict. Richa was just as happy to let someone else make the calls. Her platoon's job was to pin this front down, and that's what they would do.

A loud thunking noise startled Richa back to the present. An enemy bolt struck the cart she and her comrades were using as cover. She jumped back instinctively before calmly taking her place in the line again, returning to her work: crank, load, aim, fire, repeat. Vaguely, she hoped the other side wouldn't realize they weren't in any real danger from her direction.

As another bolt left her bow, one of her platoon mates called out, "They're moving up! A group is advancing on us!"

"Shit," Richa said, spitting just a little. After the first few battles she'd been in, it was now instinctual to make a call without hesitation. Hesitation cost lives. "Kiras, Johnnym, LeftHand, move to your right, form up, hit them with bolts as long as you can, then pull swords. Ginny, Bink, Cratius, you're with me on the left. Same deal. Ready?" She hesitated as another volley of bolts hit their cover. "Now!"

The small group rolled out and separated. After a moment of recovery, they took up positions behind such cover as they could. Richa squatted behind a tree that didn't seem big enough. A hundred yards ahead of them, a group of Loyalists moved forward carrying makeshift shields. There were fifteen, maybe twenty or more of them—nearly three times their number.

But Richa could see they were inexperienced. *They should make a wedge and rush through the killing space*, she thought to herself. But they were advancing as a tightly bunched group, at a walk. She made a grim face. It was about to get ugly.

Kiras' group started launching volleys. *Good man*, Richa thought grimly. He had seen the same weaknesses she had. From their elevated position, they were carefully placing their darts just up and over the outside edge of the grouping. Those Loyalists just behind the group with the shields would be unprotected. She adjusted the tension on her crossbow, barked a quick order to her small group to do the same, and they started firing.

Eventually the Loyalists caught on to what was happening and started a charge. But by then, it was too late. Nine were down, still and tangled on the cobblestones or dragging themselves out of the fight to die somewhere safer. Suddenly, the numbers just didn't add up. The remaining group came charging up, but again, they weren't prepared for a coordinated counter attack from two sides. Richa's sword lashed out with an experienced thrust. She had seen enough of her friends fall now to know that initiative is more than half of winning a close quarters duel. She feinted once high, then cut deep and low. The angry edge of her sword sliced through cloth, then flesh, and finally with a crack into bone. The screams of her opponent and several of his comrades filled her ears and while she kept her eyes open, she shut herself off from the grisly horror of it.

It ended. Loyalists scattered as they could. Only one in Richa's group had been injured. Four Loyalists were down, dead or dying. They had been lucky. A more experienced assault would have driven them off with losses.

Richa's instinct was to run to help the wounded men on the ground, still screaming in agony or calling out. But her platoon had to fall back under cover. Those attackers were only a small part of the larger front, meant to clear her and her friends away. Bolts started falling again as she blocked out the pleas of dying men. She could not help them, or even give them mercy. She calmed her breathing and settled back into a rhythm: crank, load, aim, fire, repeat.

"Damn it, Kiras! We call ourselves 'Arkers' but who's seen the thing lately anyway? How many of us don't even know what the name means?" Sabine turned away as she said this. After a deep breath she said softly, "We don't have the resources to feed our people, much less gaze at the heavens."

"Sabine, our people need you now more than ever. We're winning, you know." Kiras wished he was better with words. He had always been a great athlete, and in the last two years had become an excellent soldier. But he still had difficulty expressing himself. Platitudes were about as good as he could muster.

Sabine sighed. She knew all of this about her youngest general. She knew he meant well. She even believed that he thought it was true they were winning. But she knew also that he couldn't see the bigger picture the way she could. She had trained as an apprentice to a continuity elder in her early youth. Though the elders had become backward and rigidly conservative in the years before the war, she still believed the roots of their wisdom should not be lightly set aside.

She pulled the map of the Great Web out once more. It was tattered and scarred from use and age. She set books on the corners and took out several swatches of colored cloth. The green swatches she placed in a line over the Arker circles. The red, over the remaining Loyalist circles. Then with purple, she covered a distressing number of circles on the western border.

"These, Kiras," she said, pointing sharply at the purple swatches. "These are circles overrun by barbarians. This is unheard of in all the generations of the Web." Sabine paused to let that sink in. "The roads of the Web are filled with refugees. Nowhere's safe. Everyone fights. People are hungry. We must stop this."

"We're trying, Sabine. We're trying."

"No." She was firm with her young general. "You are trying to win a war. We must *stop* the war."

"You want us to give up? Surrender?" Kiras was taken aback. Surely that's not what she meant, but he suddenly wasn't sure.

"No. But it's time to reach a hand out to the elders. We need to stop bleeding. They must understand this. Their own resources must be dwindling, and no one knows better than they that this path we're on will only lead to our mutual destruction."

"Azra would be saddened," Kiras said quietly, immediately wishing he hadn't. It was a common phrase used by those who saw others drop the ball, shirk their duty. It was an insult, and it cut.

Sabine made as though she hadn't heard or felt the barb. "Open your eyes, Kiras. Azra is long dead. He lived in a world of rules and laws. A world of plenty. We live in a world of war and hunger. The empty bellies of my people are my greatest concern now." She lowered her voice and spoke in a quiet, reverent tone. "I no longer care why this war started. I've lost friends, brothers, sisters. My youngest cousin fell to a Loyalist blade on the Wall at the fifth circle East of the great forest. Cut open at the gut. She lived for five more hours. Five horrible hours of pain and torture. She was fourteen."

Kiras had been in many battles, but mention of this one turned him cold. Loyalists had set a trap for the group of Arkers who had arrived to help re-take the city early in the conflict. They had been drawn in, then slaughtered.

"I'm tired, Kiras. If we were to win the war today, who would be left to cultivate the fields? Who would rebuild our homes? It must stop. The elders know this too." She turned to him. "You will take off your General's cloak. You are now an Ambassador. It is my command, Kiras, that you go to the elders in the third circle North of the glade. Take with you only two companions—whomever you wish. Do not surrender. Do not sell us to the elders. But do not come back until the war has ended, and peace is in the land again."

Kiras rose slowly. Despite the foreboding feeling in his gut, and with the great restraint of a good soldier, he nodded to Sabine, then turned to take his leave.

They hung Kiras and his companions' corpses outside the gates of the circle. Sabine looked hard for a moment through her spyglass. Finally, she said a silent prayer for her young friend, swallowed hard, and turned to a page. "Please take a note, Galena." Her charge pulled out a pad and awaited her words with rigid respect. "Kiras failed. . . ." She stopped. "Start again, Galena.

"Kiras betrayed. Elders hostile. New instructions to follow. Hold positions." She spoke the words with a terse sadness. What instructions would she give her generals? To Galena, she said, "How many circles still have functioning wires?"

"We have three still in contact, Sir," came the reply.

It was getting harder and harder to wage a war on so many fronts with so few resources. "Send it to those circles. Send riders to the remaining." As the page hurried away, she put the spyglass back up to her eyes to once again watch her friend dangle and sway in the late evening breeze. Though the sight of it made her sick, and ache for revenge, she mostly felt painful sadness. She had foolishly believed a gesture such as this could end the war. The elders' refusal was brutal. Sabine wondered how backwards and twisted they had truly become. Then she stopped herself. Was there a general on the other side of that wall looking at her through his spyglass wondering the same? She turned her horse, and on cue her small party turned with her.

As they approached camp, Sabine remembered the days before the war. Was it possible that their communities had been so prosperous? Here, men and women huddled before campfires with little or nothing in the pots and pans suspended above. It was worse back in the Arker circles. Hunger was their enemy now. Maybe the elders did have food and supplies cached away from before the war. Tales of it were rampant in the ranks, and it made some sense. The Loyalists were playing defense as though they could afford it.

Sabine thought with little hope about devising a new strategy. They must take back the Loyalist circles. There was no other way to survive. They were stretched so very thin. It had been some time since an attack had come from the Loyalists. They seemed content to hole up behind their walls. She ran these thoughts over and over through her mind. Sabine pulled an image of the map of the Great Web into her mind. Where were the weaknesses? Where would the elders break? Where would they find food to last through winter? Who would plant crops in the spring? How many of them would be left to fight off the hordes at their borders?

Suddenly and powerfully, she wished the rift between their two sides could unbreak, could seal and mend in an instant. There would be so much more to eat if they could stop fighting. Could she surrender? End it, just like that? She thought of Kiras swaying and rotating so slowly, so frighteningly. That would be her fate, for sure, and for countless others. What kind of life was being led behind those walls? What was it like in the Loyalist circles?

And then she stopped. That was the key. "They don't have any more than we do!" she said out loud. One of her lieutenants was startled.

"Pardon, Sir?" he said.

She turned to him and smiled. "Oncer, get me. . . ." She paused, trying to think who would best understand this new idea. "Roclet. Yes. Get me Roclet." He seemed a little startled. "On the double, Lieutenant!"

Ten short days later, her generals gathered in what had become the Arker primary circle. They stood around the large wooden table with the giant map of the Great Web. Sabine stood. She spent days preparing for this meeting. The generals quieted themselves.

"Greetings," she said in the old formal way. Her audience was much younger than she'd have liked, but they returned her greeting in the same formal fashion.

"We cannot now win this war." Her words seemed to echo as they passed over her audience.

The generals shifted and murmured where they stood, but in keeping with the formality of the meeting, none spoke out loud. When they settled, she continued. "We cannot fight our way to victory. We have too little food, supplies, and soldiers. The fortifications that the elders have built around their circles are too well maintained." A few in the crowd nodded, but still they held silent.

"Now. Many of our people believe that because the Loyalists have taken this defensive posture, it means they somehow have supplies stored away to outlast any kind of siege." She stopped and looked a few of her youngest generals in the eye. To their credit, not one looked away. She continued. "I, however, don't believe this to be the case. I don't think that if we were to breach their defenses, we'd find large caches of food, medical supplies, anything at all, really." She stopped, then opened her palms for commentary.

A general in the back stepped forward. She had bright orange curls under her cap. "Sir, if this is so, than they must be as hungry and tired as we are. Why then, did they refuse our offer of peace?"

"Right. Thank you Cerena. That is the most important question of this moment. What is it like over there in their circles?" Again, she paused and looked at the map. "We've been trying so hard to figure out a weakness in their defenses, some place where if we only attacked with sufficient force, we'd break them. But what I have come to realize, is their weakness is within."

After a moment of cold silence, she went on. "I have sent our best intelligence officer on a very strange mission. He is to avoid enemy positions altogether. He will simply get inside a circle and find out what life is like. My suspicion is that what he will find will bring us the key to ending this war." She paused, then opened her stance ever so slightly, allowing for commentary.

An older general stepped forward. "What information do you expect to learn?" he said. "And then how can that possibly be of use to us militarily?"

Sabine didn't answer immediately. She closed her eyes to conjure the image of Kiras' body floating in space. "I think, Branell, that it's horrible there. I think they will be resorting to heinous measures to keep the peace. I think they're as low on food and supplies as we are, but are managing to hide it through draconian measures. I think the population there is starving, but also quivering under the bootheel of the elders. I think that anyone—soldiers, civilians, anyone—not in the upper levels of power among the elders is very very unhappy about their lot, and would relish a change." Again she stopped and looked among her generals. They were a motley group. Most carried the sunken cheeks of those who had risen to command under very hard circumstances. But they were fair. They gave and gave and gave to the soldiers under their command. How many times had one of them ordered their troops to help out in the circle when off duty? They were respected. Liked. Sabine had known no other way. Perhaps she learned it from Jaqar. Perhaps she learned it as she fought one battle after another; each time her heart breaking and mending again. She had long ago stopped hoping for victory, and begun to simply hope for deliverance from the war.

"Our weapon will be that desire for change, for reconciliation. Our weapon will be an offer of peace, a return to civil life. We don't have food to give, but we can offer to take that bootheel off their necks. And that, my friends," Sabine opened her palms to all her people in a closing gesture, "is our last, best hope."

"The continuity elders should be hanged. Their kind erased."

Sabine looked hard at Derek. He was a resistance leader from the elders' largest circle, and now a community leader in the newly reunited central circle. He was overseeing the survival of their people. He was liked and trusted, even by the Arkers. All had heard stories of his courage. She had no doubt that he had witnessed terrible suffering, and had plenty of good reasons for wanting revenge.

The elders hadn't had any more resources than the Arkers to last them through the winter. Her simple strategy of penetrating the Loyalist circles with agents who organized coordinated resistance from within was very effective. It wasn't hard. The people of those communities were in agony, and Sabine hadn't been wrong about the bootheels either. When the last of the elder's strongholds had imploded, the Loyalists proved to be in worse condition than her own people. She stood to speak as Derek sat down.

As she looked out, she knew her voice was being tolerated only because of her role in the war effort. In such a short time after, she had been responsible for decommissioning the military, but not much else. Her talents for military strategy weren't necessary any longer, and her early time studying with the elders made her suspect in some minds. *This speech isn't going to help with that.* "The elders made terrible choices, it's true," she began. "They murdered and tortured their own. Each elder who made these choices should be put before a tribunal and punished accordingly for their role. I suspect not many will escape the gallows." She stopped and looked out over her audience. High ranking officers and community leaders all gathered to decide the fate of the Loyalists and their leaders. Sabine continued, "But their order and the wisdom they kept was valuable for so very long." Dissenting murmurs echoed from the crowd, but formal respect was maintained.

"I say, we need the elders and their work. We need voices who remind us of the folly of overreaching ourselves. If the elders had done their work true to their vows, instead of selfishly seeking power, there would have been no war." Though she knew this to be an oversimplification, Sabine dropped her hands, remained standing, inviting comment.

A woman from the back of the room stood and addressed Sabine. "How would that work? Would we have to start an order from scratch with young people not indoctrinated by the criminal elders?"

Another man shouted, "Yeah, how could we trust them again?!"

Then the room broke all formality. Angry voices shouted epithets and fists shook in defiance of her words, calling for a swift end to the continuity elders. She took a step back and quickly Derek jumped up in front of her. He was calling for calm, but the audience wasn't calm. They were still shouting angrily as Sabine left by a side door. She had known her ideas wouldn't be popular. She didn't know if she was strong enough to follow through with rebuilding the order of the continuity elders. Those headwinds seemed just too strong.

She thought back to an evening, long ago, when her dear friend was close to death. Shakre had lived a long and fruitful life, working as a botanist. They had met when Sabine was just a little girl. Shakre had taken a liking to her. They drank tea together just about every afternoon. Though Shakre was a scientist, she had approved of her choice to study with the elders before she found her calling in the military. It was during this time that Shakre suddenly became ill, and had summoned Sabine. It was only a year or so after the discovery of the Ark. Shakre held Sabine's hand. Her hand had been rough and leathery, but small—shrunken almost.

Shakre closed her eyes, then opened them again, focusing on Sabine's face as though trying to memorize her features. "A very old friend told me something once, which I think I need to share with someone." She stopped to take a breath. With great effort, she continued. "I think that someone is you . . ."

Now, as the echoes of angry voices faded behind her, Sabine stepped through an ancient archway and out into a cold spring rain. She wondered if Azra was right. Was their fate to become the Ancients? Back in that small chamber with her dying friend, Sabine had promised her that she wouldn't let that happen. Sabine had promised and promised and promised again, "I won't let that happen. No matter what."

And now, was she too tired to take up her promise where no one else would? She turned the collar on her overcoat up against the rain. *Before promises can be kept,* she thought, *I must find something to eat.* She stepped down into the muddy street and faced the cold, cleansing rain.

HELIUM DISCIPLES
BY CHLOE WOODS

Surrey, England
2020

There was no fight. There was only, in the end, quiet surrender.

Eileen Cameron was 68 years old. Hours after his shift had ended Paul sat beside a narrow bed and helped her say goodbye to the world, because there was nobody else. Frail as a lost bird, fear showed in her flickering eyes and in the way her hand held tight to his, until her grip finally weakened and the morphine drip dragged her into a sleep from which she would not wake.

Paul wanted to punch the wall. Instead he filled out the necessary forms, shrugged on his jacket, and departed the great white hospital to morning twilight, where he decided it was bright enough to risk the worn path around the playing fields. He jumped across the cracked basins of dry puddles, ducked under overhanging branches and sent a blackbird chattering away into the undergrowth. There was a song, he remembered—but that had been a long time ago, and it was a lie.

Jane was fixing breakfast when he arrived home. She glared at Paul as he entered the kitchen and turned away. Paul slumped into his usual seat, opposite Kitty, who flashed him a sympathetic smile.

"You're late," said Jane. She flipped two fried eggs onto a plate, set it at her own place and leaned in to sniff Paul's coat with a disgusted expression. "Have you been smoking?"

"Good morning to you too."

"Don't start," his wife snapped. "You shouldn't let them overwork you like that. You've got to stick up for yourself. What was that for?"

This to Kitty, who had rolled her eyes. Now she gave her mother a perfectly innocent look. "Nothing."

"I hope you're going to insist on your overtime pay," Jane continued.

"I wasn't—"

"You weren't what?"

"I was at the hospital, but I wasn't—it wasn't work." Paul shook his head. "I'm sorry, I need to get to bed." He couldn't remember when he'd last slept—twenty-four hours ago—maybe twenty-six. Jane gave him a frown that suggested she was going to harangue him more later, and waved him impatiently away.

When he left the bathroom, Kitty was standing at the top of the stairs. She bit her lip, and said, "Did somebody die again?"

"Yeah."

"I'm sorry. I'm sure you did everything you could." She gave him a hug, then darted down the stairs. For a moment after the door had slammed Paul stood staring at the place where she'd been.

"No," he said quietly. "No, we didn't."

Paul could only afford a few hours' sleep, and he wasted most of them in exhausted meditation. Once, when he'd finally managed to drop off, he was woken by Jane clattering around, and he stayed very still until she went away. Later, a warm weight on his legs told Paul the cat had climbed on top of him and curled up to doze. When his alarm had been silenced Paul sat up, disturbing her, and coaxed her close again to scratch behind her black-tipped ears and let her nose around his fingers with a rumbling purr. After a few minutes the grey tabby grew bored and wandered off. So Paul had to get up.

He threw together breakfast from odds and ends in the bread bin and washed it down with coffee strong enough to make an elephant buzzed. It was past midday, the sky a burnished blue, the air so hot and still it wavered above the patio. He could see Jane through the back window. She'd gone to tinker with the barbecue, wearing loose clothes and a scarf to keep the sun off. Even with the doors wide open it was stifling in the kitchen.

Paul turned the radio on and set about chopping mushrooms to the twanging chords of a chart-topping musician he doubted he could have named under torture. Half an hour later he had a pile of chopped vegetables strung onto skewers and he was swearing at the cooker, which had clearly been designed by a lunatic: instead of buttons and dials it had an unreliable touch-screen interface, which did nothing until Paul was reduced to jabbing at it. Only then did he realise he'd used a pan the wrong size for the ring. The cooker started to beep when he lifted it away. In his frustration, Paul barely noticed that his phone—resting in its cradle at the wall sockets to charge—had started to trill at him.

He grabbed it just before it clicked over to the answer phone and accepted the call. A familiar face sharpened onto the screen. Worry replaced Paul's joy at the call when he saw how ashen his son looked, and deepened at the unusual lightness in his voice.

"Mum's got you in the kitchen, has she?" said Jack.

"I don't mind. It's too hot to work out here."

Jack laughed, mirthlessly. "Don't tell me about hot, Dad."

"All right." Paul fumbled with the pan and for something to say. "How goes it?"

"The same. Tell me—do you have any idea what K wants for her birthday?"

Paul decided not to push it. He threw out a few ideas. Kitty was easy to buy for, but it struck Paul that the ones who were easy to buy for were always the ones it was hardest to find something really special for: almost anything would please Kitty, but few things would really make her eyes light up, and fewer now she was no longer a little girl. Jack seemed to have a knack for picking the best presents for his sister. Maybe it made up for being too far away to give them to her in person. Maybe.

They talked for perhaps ten minutes, during which time Paul just about managed to get the cooker to do what he wanted, then waved goodbye. Jane had started to ferry burger patties, sausages and fat potatoes wrapped in silver foil outside and Paul was working on a trifle when Kitty returned, slammed the door and thumped upstairs. Husband and wife stared at each other.

"Jane, you don't need to . . ."

"And let her think it's acceptable to behave like that in this house?" said Jane. She whirled around and marched from the kitchen. Two minutes later the yelling started. Paul sighed, lifted the cat from the counter and turned the radio up.

Thanks to the fight, none of them were ready by the time Jane's parents arrived. With another set of parents this might not have mattered, but Chen Su and Zheng were elderly, wizened and nonetheless terrifying. They sniffed their way around the house and tutted in disapproval at the state of the barbecue, which Zheng immediately took charge of. Paul wondered if he would melt. More realistically, he was liable to set off a coughing fit from the swirling smoke; but nobody could ever tell Chen Zheng what to do, and Paul didn't try. Jane followed them outside about ten minutes later, dressed in a sleek summer dress with her hair still slightly damp in its twist.

Kitty didn't emerge until her mother went back in to chase her out. She stayed unusually silent while Su went on at length about the bin men, the buses, the cost of taxis, the cost of petrol, the government, a friend who'd voted for them and was now not being spoken to, the uselessness of shop assistants and the antics of a third cousin once removed who'd got drunk at Paul and Jane's wedding, twenty-five years ago this November, and neither of them had seen the man since. When Su started on about the health service Paul too had to bite his tongue. He caught Kitty's eye and shared an exasperated look.

"What happened?" he asked, in a low voice so as not to catch the attention of any of the Chens. "Earlier?"

"There was a march in town. Defenders. Stupid outfits and stupid signs and stupid horrible chants and we were, I guess there was a group of us, and it turned into a bit of a counter-protest and . . . there was aggro on both sides, I suppose, but there were more of them, and three of our people needed to go to A-and-E—but the police only made *us* leave. Not any of them, not even the fu— the violent ones. *They* get police protection." She jammed her fork into the paper plate.

"Wankers," said Paul, and Kitty managed a smile.

"Who was your patient? Was it bad?"

"No, not as bad as some." And he told Kitty, quietly, not about the death but what he knew about the life of one Eileen Cameron. She'd been a doctor for four decades and retired a year early when she received the diagnosis. Two sons, one overseas in the RAF, the other six feet deep on a grassy knoll where flowers grew in springtime. Her husband had left for a woman who wasn't dying. She'd had a working life of drudgery and resentment from the people she tried to help, stoked up by successive governments determined to drive nails into any notion that we should help those weaker than ourselves, followed by four years of chemotherapy, of grief, of remission and hope and recurrence and finally the damning prognosis, the sorry looks, the months alone at home waiting for the nurse followed by months in a hospital bed. Miserable little details. The way she'd insisted on doing her make-up every day. The tears of her living son, on the far end of a stretched line, the final time they spoke. The fact that her last meal had been stale hospital food.

Doctors cared, but from a distance; they were pulled so thin over all of their patients that they couldn't pay much attention to any single one for fear of giving way. It was the nurses and other staff who carried, if they could, the weight of individual lives.

Paul wondered if Eileen Cameron would have wanted her story told. She had feared dying, by instinct, but his impression was that she hadn't thought much of her life. She had known how unhappy she was and viewed her death as a chance for peace. So perhaps it was a dishonour to try to bind her to the world.

Perhaps the lie—the big, devastating, gut-wrenching thing that Paul couldn't begin to talk about, even to Kitty—wasn't, in a way, such a terrible lie at all.

He wished he could believe that.

While he told this story, the barbecue carried on and the sun edged towards the north-western horizon. They served corn on the cob with lashings of butter and vegetable kebabs. Char-grilled burgers followed, along with baked potatoes drowned in Orkney cheddar, sausages from Gloucester and garlic roasted in the red embers. Finally, Paul's trifle—of which he was justly proud: rich tiramisu, and sweet early strawberries with cream. The savoury dishes were accompanied by plenty of wine, the dessert by Pimm's and mojitos. Paul paced himself and tried to mark how much the others were drinking. Kitty had scraped her bowl clean of cream and was on at least her third glass of Pimm's by the time Su said, "Our poor lawn's wilting to nothing in this ridiculous hosepipe ban."

"It's not ridiculous," said Kitty.

Anybody else would have heard danger in her tone, but Su continued blithely, "Yes, it is—it's completely unacceptable. We pay for that water, don't we?" She looked around for support. Jane and Zheng nodded.

Jane chipped in, "It's worse here. The ruddy council put us on rations—fifty litres a day! They're talking about a standpipe in the street."

Kitty opened her mouth to say something and closed it again. Paul looked around the garden. Beyond the patio there was yellowing turf, carefully stripped of all the daisies and buttercups and clover that seemed to him the right and natural residents of even a tame lawn. One neat flowerbed ran up the left-hand side, and the boundaries of the garden were marked by varnished wooden fence in which the matching shed was almost perfectly camouflaged. Paul had suggested in the past that they could tear bits of it up and plant vegetable beds. Instead of a lawn bordered by roses he could picture twining peas and fresh potatoes to dig up, blackcurrant bushes, chickens roaming around to eat the slugs. An overgrown tangle in the corner would shelter wildlife and provide flowers for bees. But no: it was too much effort, and they could get perfectly good vegetables from the shops—all year round, *I might add*—and anyway, what would the neighbours think? The kids had grown strawberries in pots when they were younger. Paul had once thought about putting his name down for an allotment, but he was too busy with work to do it justice and would probably die of old age before he reached the top of the waiting list.

"It's not as if we've never had hot summers before," said Zheng.

"Well, it is particularly hot this year," Jane demurred.

"You're not telling me you believe all that nonsense about global warming?"

"Climate change," said Paul, too quietly for his father-in-law to notice the correction. He couldn't remember the last time he'd heard somebody refer to it as "global warming". Even people who insisted it was actually getting colder because there had been two inches of snow before New Year tended to use the accepted name—unless, of course, they were over eighty years old.

"I'm not saying I believe *all* the nonsense, but you can't admit the climate never changes. We've had ice ages in the past, haven't we? It doesn't sound all that terrible to me—how do you fancy English wine?"

"If you believe what they say on the news, it's practically the end of the world," said Su.

This time, Paul managed to make himself heard. "The bad's going to outweigh the good. In thirty or fifty years, large parts of the world are going to be unlivable. The weather doesn't just get hotter, it gets more extreme—we'll have more storms, more droughts, more winter floods." God, he sounded like a lecturer, a bored newsreader, the lines in his children's schoolbooks. *This has been a party political broadcast.* And they weren't listening.

"Well, aren't you all doom and gloom?" said Zheng. "I don't think I really need to worry about that. I mean, I'll be dead in thirty years, it's hardly as if—"

The sound of shattering glass made them all jump. Kitty, cold-eyed, deliberately held her arm outstretched for a second or two before pulling it back into herself.

"Nice to know you care, Grandfather."

"Catherine Grace Scott, what the *hell* do you think—"

Kitty ignored Jane, ignored her grandmother's hiss of disapproval, ignored everybody. She stood and walked away. Her shoes crunched on broken glass.

"Who is it?"

"It's just me."

"Okay."

Paul opened the door and leaned in the frame. Kitty sat cross-legged on the bed, her tablet in her lap, earphones strewn across the unmade duvet as if she'd hastily taken them off. A few things might have been thrown around in anger. (In Kitty's room, it was often hard to tell.) She had the cat curled up by her side.

She looked up at him. "You're not 'just' anything, Dad."

"Um. Thanks." He rubbed his eyes. "You know how to make an exit, kiddo."

"Got to know something useful," Kitty muttered.

Paul snorted and went in to sit down beside her. Kitty leaned into his hug. "I'm sorry, Dad. I shouldn't have—it was one of the nice glasses . . ."

"It doesn't matter." He gave her shoulders a squeeze. "They're pompous old windbags. I wanted to do the same myself."

Kitty forced a laugh. Then she fell quiet for a moment, before saying, "I'm scared, Dad. It feels like the world is falling apart."

Paul considered this, confident that his daughter would know he'd heard and was thinking how to reply. Finally he said, slowly, "No. The world isn't falling apart. No more than it's ever been. Come on, Yeats was writing about that a hundred years ago, and we're still here, aren't we? The end of the world is for movies. Things are just getting more . . ."

"Haggard," suggested Kitty.

"I was going to say difficult," said Paul. "Haggard." He liked the word. It evoked strain and exhaustion. A society shambling and battered around the edges.

Kitty sniffed. "I know it's not actually—save the planet—but you've got to admit, things are pretty effed up right now." Paul thought about the Defenders in their polished boots, the ways history echoed, the ways you could find yourself on the side of it you'd never expected to end up. If they called it the third world war it would be because they'd forgotten that the first two had been named for grief rather than glory. Military graves on a grassy hill and red poppies in spring, the paper poppies in November, always remember, but how can we learn from what we never understood? And at the same time ice slipped into the salt sea—

Kitty's voice distracted Paul from his thoughts. "I don't know, it's just—it's just hard."

Paul thought wryly that this was the point at which he was supposed to reflect upon how much easier it had been to soothe his daughter when she was small; but that wasn't true. Kitty had always been a child who saw and understand too much, and she'd grown up in a society woven through with fear and war. Jack would cry over skinned knees and playground fights. Kitty at the same age would stare at Paul with too-old eyes and ask if there wasn't any way to make the world better.

Now in two weeks she would graduate and in two months she would turn twenty-one and in however many months more she would leave. Fly the nest. Paul had already released his son to the wide world. He didn't feel ready to watch his daughter depart too—but she was ready to go, so he would have to be.

"I know it's hard, but what did I always tell you?"

Kitty rolled her eyes. "Life is hard."

"Actually, no. I was thinking of the other one."

His daughter frowned at him. "Um. Cheese before bed will give you nightmares? Or maybe it's, if all your friends jumped off a bridge . . ."

"Brat," said Paul. He gave her a poke. "I mean, all we need is to be kind and to love one another, and the rest will either fall into place or fall away."

"Do you really believe that? Don't you think—you know in a hundred years we'll be living in ruins if we go on like this and I don't know, I, I don't know how we stop it."

"We don't stop it. You can't fight reality, kiddo."

"That's giving up," said Kitty. A hard edge in her tone suggested she was starting to feel more like herself.

He shook his head. "I don't mean. . . . You can't fight reality. You can't change the limits of the world. That doesn't mean you can't fight people—or for them. I know it feels like they won't learn and can't learn, but that's not true, it's not—inevitable the way it is that things are going to change and we're going to have to find ways to live with it. And you, you are clever and strong and you are so much braver than me. You're going to be just fine."

"What about you? Are you happy?"

"That doesn't matter."

"Dad, of course it does."

"Kiddo, look. I love your mother. And my work, what I do—it's exhausting, it's difficult, sometimes it's heartbreaking. But last night, if I hadn't been there, then there would have been nobody to sit next to Eileen Cameron in her final moments, and offer what comfort another human being can, just so that she didn't die alone. . . . I can't even contemplate letting that happen. It has nothing to do with my happiness."

Kitty's expression was one of dawning realisation. Paul didn't ask what she thought she'd started to grasp. He had a few guesses, and probably none of them were right; most likely it was something only she could see. She was growing up.

Paul wondered what would make his daughter truly happy. He was so proud of her and at the same time he wished she wasn't so much like him. It hurt like hell to know how hard her life was going to be. All of their lives.

And she deserved to know the truth of it.

"Kitty," he said. "Eileen Cameron—she didn't have to die."

"What do you mean?"

He meant that they could have saved Eileen Cameron. Possibly. With the first round of treatment her cancer had gone into remission but the team had been lax on follow-ups, in ten years' worth of constant reorganisation nobody could keep track of. They'd caught the re-emergence too late and by then funding had been cut back so far that it wasn't considered worth wasting so much money on an old lady. In medicine there were no guarantees, but their knowledge of how to treat cancer continued to advance in leaps and ten years ago the money would have been there. Given the funding and effort available ten years ago with the technology available now, Eileen Cameron would probably have been saved.

"Saved for what?" asked Kitty.

Later, as the sky darkened, they settled down to watch the news. There was a report on the price of helium. A sunburned newsreader announced, "We have a representative here from the party industry to talk to us about the issue . . ."

"Oh, so people won't be able to have balloons at their parties," said Jane, talking over the discussion on the screen.

"It's not just balloons. We shouldn't be using helium for balloons at all. It's important for all kinds of medical things, for research, for physics," said Kitty.

"But they can make more helium, can't they?"

"Sure," said Kitty, "If you've got a trillion tons of hydrogen and a main-sequence star handy, sure you can."

"Don't be a smart-arse."

Paul tuned out the rising argument. He focused on the image flickering across the screen: a hundred brightly coloured party balloons released to the sky in some forgettable town square. Rubber from the rain forest, plastic balloon stoppers and ribbon, helium mined deep beneath the planet's surface. The image flashed to a generic scene of scientists working in a lab, then to an MRI machine.

They hadn't been able to give Eileen Cameron the MRI scans she'd needed. They were too expensive. They required helium to cool them to the low temperatures required for perfect function, and the price of helium had been rising for years. Eileen had been given CT scans instead, radioactive and less effective in examining brain tumours than the safer MRI. That was far from the only way her care had been compromised; it was impossible to say if one thing might have tipped the balance towards life. Still it made Paul sick to think of the balloons floating upwards—upwards—helium escaping from the tiny pores to float away from the planet into the depths of space. People said they would travel between the stars. No. No, they wouldn't—but they'd sent helium there.

When the fat face of the party-company executive reappeared and the man began to spout off some nonsense about the horrors of regulation, Paul could stand it no more. He stood, quietly excused himself, and left the house.

The evening was finally cooling. He walked along rows of picture-perfect suburban houses built fifty years ago to last for twenty, with neatly mown lawns and tame flower beds. A fox darted across his path. At the third corner he struck onto the playing field path where he'd left it before and continued round.

Birds sang less in summer. A set of notes caught his ear and Paul stopped to listen. The tones of the blackbird were unmistakable. They sounded like a flute—no, a flute sounded like a blackbird. The blackbirds had come first. With any luck they would still sing long after human orchestras had been forgotten.

He wondered if Eileen Cameron had found her happiness in the still moments. In the quiet details of the world: a child's laugh and the hush of waves and birdsong at twilight after a long day. In the knowledge and certainty of rest. No, there was a song, and it wasn't a lie—it was meant honestly even if it wasn't true. Freedom in death. It would be easy to believe that there had to be something better after death, but somehow Paul had never thought like that. If life was all they had then they had to fight for it, because as long as they were alive then the hope of something better remained: joy and love and help for pain.

Then again, perhaps some people didn't want hope. Perhaps they only wanted peace, and death brought it, and that was enough. If this was true then Paul thought that maybe it wasn't a lie either to say they'd done all they could for Eileen Cameron. To cure her sickness, to extend her life, how many others would have been consigned to pain and misery? He did not think she was a woman who would have wanted that. Perhaps what had been done for Eileen Cameron—in the end when there were no other choices—had even been the best thing for her. And the dead all rested the same.

It was a beautiful song. It was a beautiful bird. It was nothing and it was everything. He stood here, listening to a blackbird whistle on a too-hot summer evening, and the world turned and burned and old women died with only hospital nurses to hold their hands and at the same time birds foraged for nests full of fledglings almost ready to fly, and perhaps hope wasn't the point at all. Not hope, at least, that they could change the terrible things waiting to crash down upon the world. Not hope that they would somehow find the resources to cure all the sick people who deserved a second chance. Not hope that they'd one day be living on Mars. Maybe hope that they'd be able to face the reality of the world with dignity and courage.

Or perhaps not: perhaps they would give in to their own weaknesses and illusions, in quiet surrender, and when the dust settled there would still be blackbirds and most likely there would still be people to pick themselves up and start again.

The song ended. A rustling in the bushes told Paul the bird had moved away. He lit a cigarette and started along the path. A few stars flickered into sight overhead. Humming to himself, he went gentle into the warm night.

RED WING

BY BART HILLYER

Riggs paused to rub his aching wrist. The weird crud encasing the clapboards of the old house seemed to defy simple physics. Sweat dripped off his brow in the July sun. Riggs gazed again, as he had a dozen times that morning, at the scraper in his hand. Which would give out first? The scraper, or the crud? Or would it be Riggs himself? His rueful smile hinted at the answer.

"Why are you trying to scrape that off? Why bother?"

At first, Riggs thought that his own thoughts had somehow managed to give themselves a voice. That the voice was female was a surprise, but not a jarring one. Why not? Why shouldn't his more rational ruminations speak in a pleasing, feminine lilt?

But a slow look down from his makeshift scaffold, suspended from a second story window, revealed the source of the questions. Peering up at him was a woman he hadn't seen before. She was pretty, not too thin, youngish, barefoot, with brown hair tied in a ponytail. Her buff-colored homespun dress was given shape by a braided sash. She held a basket of cucumbers on her hip and shaded her eyes with a tanned hand missing its pinky finger. Riggs found the hand strangely endearing.

"I'm an artist," he answered her. "My masterwork will be the liberation of this house from the evil shroud that encases it." Riggs was surprised by the truthfulness of his answer, and at his willingness to offer it up to a stranger. He was surprised, also, that he knew the answer.

The young woman considered Riggs impassively. "What is that stuff? I've never seen anything like it."

"It's a high-tech coating from the late nineteen-hundreds." Both Riggs and his interlocutor smiled at his use of the term "high-tech". "People sprayed it on buildings to save themselves the trouble of painting."

Her brow furrowed slightly. "But doesn't it protect the wood from the elements? And it might even produce some insulating effect."

Riggs, coming to himself now, was self-conscious. How dirty were his clothes? How wild was his hair? He usually at least glanced in the mirror as his day began, but he hadn't this morning. "My objection to it is strictly aesthetic," he replied. "It makes the house look fuzzy—out of focus. It deserves to be seen as it was."

The woman held her injured hand before her and gazed at it. "Does my hand deserve to be seen as it was? No matter how I look at it"—she turned it this way and that—"it's still missing a finger." She turned her eyes upward again to Riggs.

The silence lengthened as Riggs considered his answer. "The loss of your finger was accidental, or so I assume, and can't be undone. The application of this goop was deliberate, and ought to be undone." Riggs paused. "And anyway, your hand suits you just as it is."

The woman smiled with sudden shyness at the awkward compliment, and looked away from Riggs. She pulled a cucumber from the basket and laid it on a stone next to the walk. As she strode away she turned back to Riggs. "That's nice and crisp. But you should eat it today." She turned away again and hastened her step. Riggs barely heard her say "My name is Lizzy" as she moved toward the market square.

II.

There wasn't much light in the cellar, just that which came through the small windows set high in the concrete walls, but it was enough for Riggs to see what he needed to see. He pulled back the coarse cloths covering the two big crocks on the trestle table and sniffed the yeasty contents. Another day or two for the blackberry, he thought, and a little longer for the peach. They were coming along nicely.

A shadow fell across the open southwest cellar window and Riggs could see someone kneeling down outside, looking through it. She spoke, and Riggs recognized Lizzy's voice. His pulse accelerated slightly. "Wow, where did you get all the big bottles?" she asked. She gestured to the shelves arrayed along the cellar wall opposite her, where about 20 five- and six-gallon clear glass containers sat stolidly. Most were full or nearly full of clear liquid, shimmering faintly in the morning light, in shades of pink and amber and lavender.

"They're called carboys," answered Riggs, "and most of them I inherited from Nick Stavos. He taught me how to make wine. When he passed away he willed them to me." Riggs stepped to the window. His eyes were just a little lower than Lizzy's. Riggs caught a whiff of lemon verbena from her dress.

Lizzy settled back on her haunches and tilted her head slightly. "Are you Mr.

Riggs?" she asked.

Riggs was embarrassed. Twice he had encountered this woman, and still he hadn't managed to tell her his name. What a knucklehead.

"It's just Riggs," he replied. "No one ever calls me mister." He wiped his hands absentmindedly on his shirt. "I apologize for failing to introduce myself before now. I know that you're Lizzy, and you live out south of town, but that's about it."

Lizzy looked to her right, toward the street where Riggs could hear a horse and wagon pass by. "I just recently came to live with my grandmother, the lady you folks call Miss Polly," she said.

Lizzy was Miss Polly's granddaughter! Everyone thought she was a spinster lady—with a name like Miss Polly, what else could you think?—but now Lizzy pops up out of nowhere. Riggs admired her for putting up with the irascible old woman. He was sure it wasn't easy.

Lizzy looked again at Riggs and asked, "Do you mind if I join you for a closer look at the winemaking operation?"

"Please do," said Riggs. "The cellar door is at the back." He moved to the door as Lizzy did the same and let her in. She stood for a moment, her basket of tomatoes and squash on her hip, as her eyes adjusted to the dim light.

Riggs regarded her intently, but politely. Up close, she looked older—thirty, maybe?—and her eyes were more wary than he had realized before.

Lizzy stepped softly to the racks of carboys. "Wow, some of these look pretty old," she said. "Is there any way to tell when they were made?"

"With some, yes," Riggs replied. He hoisted an empty six-gallon carboy from the rack, grasped it by the neck to turn it bottom-up, and held it so the light from the window struck the base. "You can see the manufacturer's mark molded into this one," he said as he pointed to a diamond shape with "O-I" inside the diamond. "That's Owens-Illinois, a company that made this at a plant in Alton, about fifty miles north. And down here"—he moved his finger under the diamond mark—"is the year they made it."

"Nineteen fifty-six!" said Lizzy. "This thing has been around for more than a hundred and fifty years! Are they all that old?"

"Some are older still," said Riggs, "but most manufacturers didn't bother with markings like this. Too much trouble and expense. But Owens-Illinois was big—the biggest in the world—and they wanted to tell the world." Riggs turned the big bottle right side-up and set it down again. "Can you imagine the gigawatts it took to make molten glass and mold these bottles, hundreds or thousands in a run, for hours and days and weeks on end? What a time that must have been!"

Lizzy frowned. "Well, they used up the juice mighty quick, I'll give them that. Seems like they might've saved a bit more than they did for all the folks who came later."

Riggs rubbed his chin reflectively. "Well, I don't know. I've thought about it a lot. They probably just figured if they didn't use it up themselves, someone else would, someplace else. And what would be the point of letting that happen?" Riggs cracked his knuckles nervously and smiled. "Anyway, nothing goes away forever, Lizzy. There's a fellow over near Breese who salvaged some molds and now he hand-blows bottles nearly this size. I even helped him, once. Who knows, maybe they'll master fusion power one of these days, and he'll be as big as Owens-Illinois ever was!"

They both laughed. "If I didn't know better I'd think you were a cornucopian," said Lizzy. "But really, what do you do with all this wine, Riggs? Is it strictly for your own consumption or does it serve some other purpose?"

Smiling, Riggs replied, "Oh, it's just for me." After Lizzy tucked her chin slightly and regarded him skeptically, Riggs continued, "Actually, I trade most of it for things I need, or give it away. Would you like to try some?"

Lizzy smiled broadly. "I thought you'd never ask. What do you recommend?"

Riggs opened the door of an old wardrobe to reveal shelves crowded with glass wine bottles, earthenware jugs and canning jars, all apparently full. After considering for a moment he chose two standard wine bottles filled with pale reddish-purple fluid and pulled them out. "This is blackberry from a couple of years ago," said Riggs. "It's just about my favorite." He lifted one bottle and then the other. "One for us and one for you and Miss Polly. The corkscrew is upstairs."

Riggs stepped to the open staircase and let Lizzy ascend first. They emerged into the kitchen, bright and cheery in the morning sun, where Riggs pulled out the corkscrew and two small jelly-jar glasses. He removed the cork from the bottle with a satisfying *thunk* and poured out about a half-cup into each glass.

Lizzy took hers and sniffed the contents delicately. "A very nice aroma, Riggs." She took a sip. "Wow, this is good. Like liquid velvet. How do you keep yourself from plowing through the inventory?" Lizzy arched her eyebrows as she waited for his response.

"That's not one of my weaknesses, luckily," replied Riggs. "I just have a couple of glasses a day."

Lizzy, glass in hand, had wandered from the kitchen, past the woodstove, into what was once the dining room. It was now, together with the adjacent parlor, a library, with hundreds and hundreds of books, floor to ceiling, on shelves that were homemade, but rudely handsome. In the center of the sunny parlor was a worn leather sofa with a low table before it. "Riggs, you're a bibliophile, or possibly just a librarian," said Lizzy. She ran her finger along the backs of a few dozen volumes, staring intently at them as she did. "It's an eclectic gathering, for sure. How-to, history, fiction, biography, self improvement, reference works—did you inherit these from Nick, too?"

"Only a few," replied Riggs. "About half came from my dad, and most of the rest I traded for in St. Louis, back when I was young and stupid and thought I was immortal. It was pretty self-indulgent, really. Who needs all these books?"

"Don't apologize for being yourself," said Lizzy. "Books are wonderful! They're the best way humans have to communicate across time and space." She sat on the sofa, took another sip of blackberry wine, and crossed her legs. There was nothing overtly sexual about it, but Riggs was stirred as he hadn't been for a long time. "So, Mr. Librarian, who's your favorite author?"

Riggs thought for a moment. "I guess I'd have to say Jane Austen," he said. "Her stuff is real predictable, but I love the dialogue. I wonder if anyone ever actually talked that way."

Lizzy set her now-empty glass on the table and smiled. "Probably not," she said, "but I'm glad to learn that you're a romantic. So am I." She got up, walked to his side, and kissed him softly on the cheek. "I have a terrible suspicion that you're just as innocent and noble as Jane Austen's men were. I commend you for it."

Riggs's eyes shone with longing. He could say nothing in reply. Lizzy moved back to the kitchen and stood with her back to the sink. "But now down to business," she said. "Believe it or not, my visit has a purpose beyond mooching a glass of wine and quizzing you on your literary taste. Granny says I snore, which is a foul and contemptible lie, but she has directed me to hire you to build a lean-to onto her cabin. She says you aren't the most talented handyman around, but you're diligent and less of a chatterbox than most men. Will you take the job?"

Disappointed at the practical turn in the conversation, Riggs was silent and slightly crestfallen for a moment. But he brightened at the thought that he could at least be near Lizzy as he did the job. "How big a lean-to?" he asked. "And what does Miss Polly want it sided with?"

"Eight by twelve," replied Lizzy, hands on hips. "Granny says she has enough old pine boards in her pole barn for clapboard siding, but you're to procure lumber for the framing."

"Sure, I'll take the job," said Riggs. "I'll round up the lumber and have Ben Wallace drop it out there day after tomorrow. And I'll be there the day after that."

Lizzy moved toward the kitchen door. "So what's your price, Riggs? Granny will want to know."

Riggs smiled. "Now you're pulling my leg, Lizzy. Miss Polly knows perfectly well that my price is whatever the customer wants to pay after the job is done."

Lizzy laughed, a deep, satisfied laugh that made her eyes crinkle. "Yes, that's what Granny said, but I didn't believe her." She picked up the unopened wine bottle from the counter and put it in her basket. Then she put several tomatoes and squash on the table and pulled open the kitchen door. "I don't know how you've managed to struggle along so far, Riggs. God must be looking after you. Thanks for the wine." She pulled the door closed behind her and was gone.

III.

Riggs checked his measurements one last time and began sawing the two-by-fours before him. The smell of the sawn pine was sweet and clean. He would've preferred two-by-sixes for the rafters of a lean-to, even this little one, but these studs were all he could find on short notice. And Miss Polly, characteristically, was in a hurry. She wanted a lean-to added to her shack, and by God she wanted it yesterday. Riggs felt a little light-headed.

Lizzy was weeding the cucumbers and tomatoes, some fifteen yards from Riggs as he stood in the shade cast by Miss Polly's cabin. The morning heat was just beginning to take hold. There was a buzzing in his ear, but when he swatted at it, Riggs could detect no insect present. He ran the back of his hand across his forehead and squinted his eyes shut.

"Why are you sawing those by hand?" The querulous voice interrupted his thoughts as Miss Polly approached Riggs from behind with her little sparrow-steps, dragging a rusty child's wagon behind her. She held her walking stick as if to strike him. "Why don't you use this?" With a flourish, like a salesman showing off a wonderful new gizmo, she used the head of the stick to pull a scrap of burlap from the bed of the wagon to reveal an old hand-held electric circular saw beneath it.

Riggs picked it up admiringly. "Craftsman" he said as he read the name stamped into the motor housing. It was one of the really old ones, with a body not of plastic but of cast aluminum. The black cord with a two-pronged plug dangled on the ground. Riggs moved the blade with his thumb. The movement was stiff, but Riggs thought it was from long disuse, not a failure of the bearings. Not that he was any expert.

"This is a nice piece of machinery, Miss Polly," said Riggs. "But how are we going to fire it up? Do you have a generator out here? And fuel? Ethanol, maybe?"

"Stop asking all these fool questions, you nitwit. You stick that thing"—she gestured at the plug—"into the wall socket and away you go! Even a feebleminded child knows that."

Riggs considered Miss Polly's outburst carefully. He knew he had to tread lightly.

"Maybe that was the way of it when you were a young lady, Miss Polly," he replied. "But these days we have to sign up for a dollop of juice at the next generation day in town. And it comes pretty dear." Riggs swayed a little as he spoke.

The obstinate old face crinkled in annoyance at Riggs's objections, but she didn't dispute them. "Hang the expense! I've got silver!" Miss Polly pulled a little leather pouch from somewhere inside her shapeless dress and shook it up. Sure enough, Riggs heard the silvery tinkle of old, old dimes.

"Miss Polly, you oughtn't to let folks know that. There's still thieves about."

Riggs felt the first stab of sticky heat behind his eyes. His throat was dry.

"Let 'em come," cackled the old woman. "I've got silver and lead both!" Reaching into yet another fold of the dress, she pulled out an old .38. The bluing was almost gone, but Riggs could see the coppery tips of the bullets in the cylinder. They were all too easy to see since Miss Polly was pointing the pistol right at him, like Bonnie Parker sitting on a Ford fender in those old photos. Her eyes were bright with purpose. Lizzy, kneeling among the tomato vines, observed her closely with sidelong glances.

Riggs closed his eyes and ran his free hand through his hair. His thoughts thickened and blurred. Was there nothing this old biddy didn't have in that lumpy dress? He imagined her pulling out six scrapers with six hands, Vishnu-like, and de-crudding his entire house in a few minutes.

His tongue was a furry lump inside his mouth. His head tilted back between his shoulder blades. "I need to gather my tools and get on home." That's what Riggs said, but all that Miss Polly heard was an incomprehensible mumble. With jerky urgency, Riggs dropped the old power saw on the ground and packed his tools in his worn canvas bag and began walking the three miles back to town. His gait was stiff and fussy, like a marionette whose operator was indifferent to actual human motion.

Miss Polly watched in disbelief as Riggs moved off. "Where in the Sam Hill do you think you're going, you lunatic? Get back here and finish the job!" She cocked the pistol with both hands and took jittery aim at his back as Riggs reached the raggedy copse of trees and undergrowth near the road, some sixty yards from the cabin. Miss Polly's index finger tightened on the trigger. Lizzy hastened over from the garden and tried to hit Miss Polly's arm as the hammer fell. The shot reverberated in their ears as Riggs and his tools collapsed noisily into the brush.

"That boy wasn't right in the head," said Miss Polly.

"You're a fine one to talk!" yelled the younger woman as she dashed into the old woman's shack. She emerged a moment later with a satchel of clean towels and sheets. "He's got more of his marbles than a certain elderly lady I know. And now he's lying there in the weeds, bleeding to death, thanks to you!"

"Nonsense!" said Miss Polly, obdurately, as Lizzie ran toward the motionless Riggs. "Just a warning shot!" the old woman called after her. "The rounds always go where I want them to go." Miss Polly's face was serene; Lizzy's worried.

IV.

The morning sun shone on the wall opposite his bed as Riggs came to consciousness. The hot needles behind his eyes were almost gone, and the throbbing aches in his joints were receding again into memory. And, most tellingly of all, he felt hungry. The worst of the malaria attack was over.

Riggs looked down at the robe he was wearing. He couldn't remember putting it on, or taking off his old clothes, for that matter. He didn't even recognize the robe.

Riggs ran his hand over the nubby sheet. It was crisp and clean, so somebody had changed the bed linens at least once since it began. On one previous occasion, about three years ago, the wife of Riggs' upstairs tenant had looked after Riggs while he was bedridden, but she had found the experience insufficiently rewarding to try again. And even then, she hadn't changed his sheets. The current situation was just a mystery.

Riggs closed his eyes again. Through the open window he could pick out the songs of sparrows and robins and finches. The whir of a hummingbird near the petunia patch. A horse's whinny. Someone hammering nails. A child's voice, hollering at a playmate. Nothing out of the ordinary. It was wonderful to lie here these few minutes, on clean sheets, in his own house, feeling better again. He said a silent prayer of thanks, awkwardly. Riggs tried not to bother the Lord excessively, one way or the other.

Suddenly a new sound appeared. It was a scraping noise in or on the house, near the back. A squirrel in the gutter or downspout? No, there was no metallic note to it. A mouse, scampering along inside the frame walls of the old house? No, the sound was too heavy and insistent.

Then it hit him. He got out of bed and stepped gingerly to the window. Sticking his head out, he looked down the north side of the house to see Lizzy, standing on a chair, scraper in hand, laboring away at the clapboards. Flecks of the strange coating were fluttering to the ground, like a little space-age snowstorm.

The remaining fuzziness in his head, or perhaps something else, made it difficult for Riggs to think clearly. He managed to say, "Persistent stuff, isn't it?"

Lizzy smiled as she turned to him. She stepped down off the chair, placed the scraper on the seat, and walked to the window where Riggs stood. "It certainly is. But it'll give way eventually--to a true artist, that is." Hands on hips, she looked up at him intently. "So, it's back to being you now, is it? I'm glad you're feeling better again."

"So am I," said Riggs. "But I'm sorry to put you to the trouble of looking after me. The malaria hits about once a year, though some years I get lucky and it doesn't come at all." Riggs paused. "How did you manage to change the sheets?"

Lizzy laughed, a wonderful, melodic laugh. "That's an old nurse's trick my mother taught me. It's not hard to learn. The real challenge was getting you to swallow some water now and again." She brushed a wisp of sun-lightened brown hair from her forehead. "I bet you're famished, but I'm ready. I went to Granny's house yesterday and picked up some eggs. And I have a little bread from the lady upstairs here. And some ham from your cellar. A few minutes over the rocket stove and we'll be ready to eat." She moved toward the back of the house, picking up the chair and scraper as she went. "I'll see you in the kitchen in a few minutes." She paused a moment and added, "I feel terrible that Granny took that shot at you. But I'm glad she missed."

Riggs moved slowly to the closet to find clean clothes. So the old woman *did* fire at him! He had thought the memory was just an artifact of his fevered dreams, but it was real. He wondered if Miss Polly was getting dangerously out of hand. Less than a year earlier, she had plugged a fellow she said had tried to steal her bicycle. That story seemed a little unlikely—the bicycle was rusty and immobile, and would have made for a plodding getaway—but no one could identify the dead man, whose pockets were suspiciously empty, and the sheriff finally decided to bring no charges. Was it safe for Lizzy to live out there with the old woman in her belligerent, perhaps murderous, mental state?

So his thoughts ran as Riggs combed his hair in the bathroom mirror and worked up a lather with his shaving brush. The price of safety razors was coming down, but they were still too pricey for the frugal Riggs. He stropped his straight razor on the leather strap hanging from the wall, and shaved carefully. From the length of the beard he cut, he surmised the attack had lasted two days.

Riggs moved closer to the mirror and gazed intently at the clean-shaven face before him. It was much the same as ever, angular with high cheekbones, deep-set pleasant brown eyes, but with a few more crinkles here and there. He was 36 now, nearly 37. No spring chicken, he told himself.

The enticing smell of ham and scrambled eggs filled his nostrils as he entered the kitchen. Riggs inhaled deeply and sat at the old pine table as Lizzy served him a fair facsimile of an old-fashioned farm breakfast. There was even a little pot of tea, presumably brewed from Riggs's stash of the precious stuff.

"I hope you don't mind about the tea," said Lizzy. "I found it in one of the cupboards and couldn't resist." She poured steaming cups for Riggs and herself.

"Not a bit," said Riggs as he surveyed the table, mouth watering. "It's always worth celebrating when the malaria fades out again, but usually I do it alone." With a shy glance at Lizzy, he added, "And with you here there's even more reason to celebrate."

Lizzy's cheeks colored a little, possibly, as she sat down catty-corner from Riggs. "So just where did you pick up malaria, Riggs? I didn't think it was widespread in southern Illinois. Do you have a mysterious past as a pirate in the tropics?"

Riggs swallowed a bite of ham and eggs, washed it down with tea, and smiled. "Nothing so exciting, I'm afraid," he replied. "It's a little leftover from our last grand national adventure, in Brazil. I signed up because I didn't have anything better to do, and two years later I was back home with a disability pension. Not bad for an ignorant country boy." He speared another forkful of ham and eggs and chewed contentedly.

"Were you in combat there?" asked Lizzy.

"Some," said Riggs. "Enough to be grateful to have it behind me." He shook his head slowly. "I have to say it's overrated." He sipped his tea. "So what brought you here, Lizzy? And from where?" He looked at her expectantly.

"I was living in Utah with my husband Dave"—she glanced at Riggs—"when he was taken by the flu. That was about a year ago. My plan was to stay there, on his brother's ranch, where Dave had lived his whole life. But Dave's idiot brother, Brigham, took the whole polygamy thing way too seriously—there's a lot more of that there these days—and insisted that I either join the harem or leave." She sipped her tea and shrugged. "So I left. Packed my worldly belongings in a little carpetbag and came to join Granny. At least Brigham paid the train fare, the jerk."

"I'm sorry you were widowed, Lizzy," said Riggs. "I hope that things are"—he groped for the right word—"acceptable to you at Miss Polly's place."

Lizzy knitted her brow as she thought. "Acceptable," she said. "I guess things are—acceptable—for now. But I don't think Granny is overly fond of company." She took another sip of tea. "Maybe the lean-to will help." She smiled archly at Riggs. "If it ever gets built, that is."

"I promise to get at it day after tomorrow," said Riggs, "if Miss Polly doesn't cut me down." He paused and fiddled with his fork. "Incidentally, it might be best not to mention her last shot to anyone else. After she killed that fellow last year, the sheriff might start thinking about locking her up in the county home, and I'd hate to see that."

Lizzy gathered the dirty dishes and moved to the sink. "So Granny really did kill a thief!" she said. "She told me so, but I thought she made it up."

Riggs and Lizzy stared thoughtfully at one another, she standing with her back to the sink, he sitting at the kitchen table. There was plenty for each to think about.

V.

"I'm very flattered at the offer, Riggs—it was sweet of you to make it. But I think you'd be miserable." Lizzy sat close to him on the pine bench and sniffed delicately at the corsage on her wrist. "I'm hard—hard through and through." The fiddle player launched into "Red Wing" and was soon joined by the dulcimer and guitar players. Several couples moved to the plank dance floor on the town square. "Before long, you'd be wishing you had Granny's boldness with a revolver." She playfully pointed her index finger at Riggs and pantomimed the fall of a pistol's hammer with her thumb.

Riggs laughed and took another sip from his wooden cup. He generally preferred hard cider, but he was sticking with the soft stuff tonight. He wanted a clear head. He set the cup down in the grass and took her hands in his.

"You're about as hard as a week-old puppy, Lizzy, and you know it," replied Riggs. "Why not just give in and admit that this is our best shot at being happy? I love being with you, and talking to you, and thinking about you. Let's face it—I love you. Just accept it. Let it be." Moonlight played across his face as the breeze stirred the leaves of the old oak tree spread out above them.

"I can't do it to you, Riggs," she replied, her eyes locked on his. "But we'll always be the best of friends."

Suddenly, all of his fears, of her and of his desire for her, left him. Calm and self assurance descended upon him. He felt as he had before combat, when the anxiety and agitation had been replaced by resolve, and confidence that he knew what had to be done.

"You're right, Lizzy, we will always be the best of friends," he said with a smile. Lizzy's lips tightened. Riggs continued. "But first we'll get married."

After a pause, Lizzy tilted her head back and laughed, a laugh that rang like a glass bell. "All right, Riggs. First, we'll get married." She turned her head slightly and exaggeratedly blew out a long breath of relief. "Thank heavens you pressed on, like a good soldier, through my ridiculous objections. But I had to make them, to save face after throwing myself at you these past weeks."

"Throwing yourself at me!" said Riggs. "Why, we haven't even had a decent kiss yet."

Lizzy had a mischievous gleam in her eye. "We're going to fix that right now, Riggs, right here on the Mascoutah town square, right in the middle of the harvest hoedown." Each pulled the other close. The dancers applauded as the last notes of "Red Wing" faded in the soft night air, and Riggs and Lizzy shared a long, satisfying kiss.

Spyne Drift

by G. Kay Bishop

A MANY NATIONS TALES

"Bring me something funny," my sister signed. "I'm bored to shards and flinders with everything in our 'lie-berry,' as the eggs call it." Eggs is my sister's code name for local yokels.

My chances of finding something good and funny for her had been lately improved. As of the 3rd of the month, *Monograph 143: On the Successful Treatment of Spinal Meningitis by Sequential Application of Herbal Infusions, Extracts, and Tinctures* was complete. I was to have the honor of taking the second replica to the Hitchins Library—said to contain more than a million books—located some 400 miles down mountain.

Well, 436.2578 miles, to be precise. On foot. Hitch-hiking, or rail-riding if I had the chance, but otherwise, all on shank's mare. We could not possibly afford passage on the aluminum company's Foiler barges. I would be lucky to have enough jujubes to pay for a few ferries and bridge tolls. On the return trip, if the weather turned ugly before I got home, I would just have to lump it.

The honor (such as it was) of being entrusted with this task would never have come to me in the ordinary course of human events. So singly important an errand would naturally have fallen to a Chief's Scribe and Second Apprentice—First 'Prentice being left behind as Acting Scribe during the others' absence. They would have taken the mules, gone down and come back in good time last autumn.

But the best laid plans are gang aft agley—and it was a pur wee mousie who landed me in the prime spot. I'll get to the mouse in a minute. But first one thing and then another ganged good and agley.

Last summer, the author of the monograph, our eldest herbalist, had a mild stroke. She recovered remarkably fast, considering all, and finished the monograph in manuscript. Then the original manuscript had to be transcribed by both apprentices—once by hand, once by manual typewriter, each copy serving as a check on the other's reproduction, and the whole to be overseen by my grandmother, the Grammarian. The Grammarian had to be coaxed, persuaded and, in the end, ordered (by the Chief, no less!) to have anything to do with a godless book of so-called science.

Being still a minor, a mere boy, I was not allowed, of course, to attend the closed Men's Council where the judgment to publish was made. I have since been given to understand that the volume was given consideration in light of its power to mitigate the stark severity of our political profile. It might redeem us ever so slightly in the Great Eye of the General Public. Even a moderate redemption for our denomination was not easy to achieve. We are a feisty lot! My grandmother was no exception.

It was never clear to me whether I was chosen as a sop to Grandmother's pride or a punishment for her obstinacy. Maybe neither—maybe I was the hostage to the book's safety while it was in her hands. It was to be my service mission to deliver the book. If the book were to be altered, harmed or destroyed, all the opprobrium of failure would fall upon me, last bearer of my father's name and his father before him.

You know, I just thought of that. It has a subtle odor of probability about it. Sly old devils, those Chiefs!

But it took that kind of leverage to dislodge my formidable forbear from any position she had once occupied, fortified, entrenched and defended with passage of arms or Scripture.

Between summer and autumn all hands were on deck. Pardon my naval metaphor for a land activity. "What's horticulture?" said Sinbad the sailor. No, never mind, that's too rude. While reaping and canning were in the fo'csle, literary efforts were consigned to the poop. Come winter, our oldest herbalist suffered a respiratory infection and, despite careful treatment, fell into a decline. All February, during her last illness, the scribes were sticking close to her as burrs on a rabbit, taking turns recording her utterances.

The scribes attended Elder Herbal day and night, in two-hour alternating shifts. We feared lest she should let fall from her lips some sovereign remedy or crucial caution about wild mushroom preparation that had not yet been transmitted to her apprentices. Important emendations and footnotes were gleaned from the stubble of her mind. The monograph would have to be corrected. Then there would be the retyping, re-binding, and, oh! save us holy father!

Only then was it discovered that mice had chewed through the sealed plastic in which our very last typewriter ribbon was stored and allowed it to dry out beyond use. They also chewed through the ribbon loop and unwound it, using the fabric for an inky nest. The ribbon mishap meant it took longer to make the copy and longer to proofread it. Both scribes had to finish the last few pages of the amended copies in a neat, cursive script, using a hastily prepared solution of oak gall ink. Plus, our Grammarian had been either balky or busy, alternately. Time was running short.

The Annual Council was fast approaching—an event that would require the combined efforts of all our scribes. They could not be spared for a long journey south. There was no time to fetch another ribbon cartridge and no one to send.

Except me.

The original plan was much simpler. I, being of least use in the field, was to carry the casings and old ribbons with me, drop them off at a good mender's mart—a reliable one!—and fetch back replacements—from Vermont only. No cheap substitutes, but the original makers. It would only take me five days to a week to get to Cedarville and I could start right away.

But heavy rains cut off the Holler from the outer world. Bridges were washed out. Spring planting came and went. More rains. Second Spring planting.

Another delay was occasioned by good intentions. Hoping to use barter to partially defray the considerable cost of re-inking ribbons, my sister wove three blank ribbons of exceptionally fine silk on her minute inkle loom. This took time, but since it took place during a spell of foul weather, I was rather glad of the holdup.

We roughed up one of the ribbons on one side with a an old emery board and carefully ironed the other side flat and smooth. It took up our improvised ink with admirable thirst and made a good impression when held tensioned between two fingers (mine) while the typist cautiously struck the keys. It seemed that the homemade ribbons needed only to be steeped in good ink, re-wound into the ribbon casings and sewn into a closed loop.

Though we were elated at our limited success, we soon had to admit defeat. The casings were sealed, one piece moldings. What we could see of the ribbon advancement mechanism was also discouraging. We had no tools for that kind of precision work, with delicate springs and thin metal flanges, nor the knowledge either. So we had to fall back on purchase. By now, hay harvest was in full swing and every mount, every wagon was in use. Even the donkeys were busy.

The several delays in preparing the manuscript were unfortunate on two counts: one, because it meant the weather might be bad for my return journey; and two, because it meant I was the one to be sent. I was considered too young, too scatterbrained, and untrustworthy for such a precious commission. Not to mention being short-sighted and undersized. At 14, I was small for a man and not likely to grow too much bigger.

My spine, it seemed, had a will of its own. It was apt to drift sideways. There were these Procrustean treatments, some of which I had before my parents died in a one-two punch of storm at sea and resistant pneumonia at the Norfolk naval hospital. But when both of my folks died in service, my health care privileges died with them. At the age of 13, I was, alas, a trifle too young to volunteer, so my sister and I wound up here, under the eagle-eyed aegis of the Grammarian of Grandville County.

I was more mole-eyed than eagle. However, I was a pretty fair navigator, if someone else took the sightings and I only had to do the calculations.

"He's no scout," my tutors and counselors said of me. I knew they were right.

"He doesn't have to be," said my Advocate, with superb unconcern. "He will be taking the Trader's Trail." Everyone knew that the Trader's Trail was so well marked it could be

followed by a blind hog and a deaf snake. So long as I stayed on it, I could not get lost and I should be quite safe, even without weapons or an escort or even a map.

Traders were considered under the protection of all peoples. Otherwise, their function would become too costly. Most merchants could not afford an armed escort; the Trail could not afford to feed large groups going to and fro. Gradually, traditions from the past came to be reestablished. Traders were not to be attacked, no tolls were to be levied on them and they were not to be employed as spies.

The first of the Traders' Trails was blazed through all territories signatory to the New Dominion Free Trade Rules. It had wide easements on both sides (to be considered neutral ground) and included some stretches of the French Broad where a solitary peddler could canoe or ferry cost free, from either bank. Ever wonder why a river bank doesn't charge interest? Because the currents, see, are dirt cheap. Ha, ha, ha.

I was no fighter either. At the time, the pun was my deadliest weapon. With it, I had slain my thousands and tens of thousands—metaphorically speaking. Luckily, all who walked the Traders' Trail were required to go unarmed. Most carried nothing more deadly than a kitchen knife, though some of them sported miniature replicas of the Arkansas toothpick for their camp knives. Mine was a more serviceable, stout broad-blade with a curved tip for can-opening. It would do.

All-Region FTR peddlers received a license in the form of a special tattoo. Civil Couriers, Post Officers, County Agents and Medical Personnel all had their own badges and uniforms. Whereas Irregular Emissaries, like me, were obliged by intercounty law to distinguish themselves by wearing special clothing (orangey-pink or sickly greenish-yellow, with ruffles and lace and frilly bits of ribbon—rather silly looking) and uniquely identifying sash bands, woven or embroidered. My sister made mine—it was a beautiful thing in colored silks. Of course, since I bred the white mulberry trees and raised the worms myself, I consider I had some stake of pride in this object d'art.

Food caches and cisterns had been set up all along the Trail, and shelter was to be had with relations or friends. I was roundly strictured to abjure all taverns, inns, and hostels.

Bedbugs, fleas, rancid butter, spoiled and fly-blown meats, tubercular milk and much worse might be expected from those unclean haunts, including, but not limited to: personal rape, political riots, impious language, lewd dancing, vile plots, disease, drunkenness, thieves, sex workers with an eye to extra profits from rolling (or even enslaving) hapless idiots such as myself, and on up to actual murder for the sake of my well-made, cork-lined, thick-soled leather shoes. Bad men and worse women were the rule, not the exception.

The police in some counties might be as bad or worse than the low-born habitues of these vicious dens. Why, I asked, should traders be given safe passage and rights-of-way, yet be denied safe shelter and harborage of their goods in transit?

"Because people are scum," was the short answer. The long answer enlarged upon this pithy motif in greater depth and detail with intriguingly Rococo variations upon the main theme, having mostly to do with usury, brigandage, and profit-making in general. While rich in information, this reply somehow failed to answer my question. You know how it is with bratty teenaged boys like me—we are just *never* satisfied. We have to learn everything the hard way, don't we? Or, so I have been reliably informed.

If all friends, relations, pastors of our particular flock, and random shepherds' huts failed me, I had been given six coils of copper wire, sewn into interior pockets in the lining of my vest and one more in the tongue of my shoe. I could, as a last resort, trade for food and lodging at a limited number of Young Widows Christian Boardinghouses; they were known to accept copper wire for their jewelry crafters' co-op. But not all of them were suitable for any relation of the Grammarian of Grandville County. I would have to use my judgment—such as it was—to decide which ones were modest enough to be suitable for a descendant of a fine family, however impoverished by untoward circumstances.

In accordance with my rank, my emissarial habiliments were required to be of an especial sartorial splendour. The shirt alone could make the devil blush. Its grace notes and embellishments were statistically compounded of an unholy assortment of thrice-mended lace, retired hair-ribbons recalled to emergency active service, heavily embroidered inset shoulder patches of sateen and velveteen, together with a knee-high heap of worn-thin calico dishtowels, just about fit for the ragbag before they achieved apotheosis as ruffles in my glorious garb.

Though she's prettier than me, Sissy is no beauty. But Lawd-help-us, can she sew! A superb tailor, a deft needlewoman and an accomplished weaver, she found her calling early in life. She had no difficulty conforming my road clothes to my peculiar shape.

Despite a dearth of fine cambric, she managed to gussy-gasket me out in so many frills, furbelows, and flounces as may never have been seen since the courts of one of the Louis's of France—I forget which. For a foundation fabric she chose slubby silk homespun seconds, warm and sturdy, but no prize-winner for the Grandville Fair.

Nor, indeed, suitable for a prince of the realm. Not many princes of the realm would willingly don a homespun suit dyed sugar beet pink. George IV of England might have been so persuaded—but only to win a bet.

The warm, cozy lining of this elaborate dress was a felt-like substance made of boiled lambswool. Sissy pieced it together from the Memory Chest: baby blankets made for dead infants, such as my mother's lost lambs, and those of other women in our church. The Memory Chest was so full, Sissy thought no one would notice if a few were missing. She took care to select the ones that belonged to our lineage.

For the great occasion, I had also a newly woven set of linen underclothes to supplement my quotidian quota. Stiff they were, though not so scratchy as tow. Sissy pounded and scraped and mangled them over and over to soften them enough for comfortable wear. If there ever was a pipterino of a gal, she's it.

Golden September was a week underway before I was. By most reckonings, it would take me a month to arrive and another to return. No one would expect to see me before First Frost or even Forebears' Feast. An effing long time, in either case. Twenty days one way was the least amount of time I could expect to travel, unless I fell in with some good luck along the way.

And my luck was in, at least for the first half of the distance. On Day One I did not have to walk more than five miles before I fell in with some Barrow Folk—a good-natured lot whose big, center-wheeled barrows were drawn by donkey teams here in the highlands and by oxen in the flatlands. They had just off-loaded a large shipment of tobacco (plugs and cigars), cheap cotton cloth, dried peaches, tamarinds, lemon peel and sea salt. They had a few miles to go before on-loading a return shipment of whiskey, woolens, linens, lisle thread, raw silk scarves, turpentine, and linseed oil.

Nothing loath to make a little extra margin, one fellow traveller accepted my smallest coin in exchange for a ride in an empty barrow, at least as far as the next halt. The Folk knew by my rig-out that I was poor and by my hat that I would not engage in any gambling (our sect was quite strict), so they asked me to sing for them to pass the time.

I knew pretty well what the response at home would have been to a heathen request for the singing of hymns as an idle, make-loose pastime: an ear-blistering homily, possibly accompanied by percussive effects from belaboring any shoulders within reach of an ebony cane with an ivory handle. Real elephant ivory, I am sorry to say, but quite old, I believe. From a time long before they became extinct.

I was under the impression that mine hosts would not have minded in the least had I refused to sing, puffed myself up like a billy-bantam, and rated them with scalding scolds from bowsprit to poopdeck—anything for a laugh, eh? They could have retailed the story of my frilly-folly and be-ribboned berating for hard cash in some town further south.

But I was not reared from my tender youth in my present household—only put there lately by misfortune's chance; and so I mildly complied with their asking. If I were to be ridiculed, at least let it be for my singing and not for my preaching.

Still, if any rumor of my unchurchly behavior should boomerang back to smite me upside of the noggin, I had better have a good story ready. In truth, I thought no harm in giving my benefactors a rousing rendition of "O! Praise Ye the Lord."

After all, praise is praise, nyetski? I could always say that I was preaching by stealth in having selected a song that elevates spiritual riches above worldly goods. And the words were set to a tune already widely known as a folk melody (formerly a drinking song), so I would be giving away no secrets of the covenant, nor violating the trusthold of the flock.

> *O! Praise ye the Lord! For all ye are worth*
> *Is naught in His reckoning; o'er all the earth*
> *No wealth ye may find save which doth the soul bind*
> *and cast into Hell for Be-el-ze-bub's mirth.*

Yes, it goes on like that for some time, with some really ripe depictions in Stanza 4 of the fate awaiting the rich man at the hands of Satan's cross-tempered angelic minions. I believe some of these are derived from dear Dante Alighieri's fertile imagination. I got three good miles of for'ard distance with the Barrowers before they turned into a lane to on-load their down-mountain cargo.

I only had to walk another mile before coming into a small town. After an interval of refreshment at the well with an apple and a bite of cheese and crackers, I was taken up for free by a farmer in a milk wagon, heading for home with a bedful of musically clanking empty cans. He declined my offer of payment with a deprecating wave of the hand, but asked if I could rattle him off a good tale to while away the hours.

Surprisingly, he and his son seemed to have read everything De Maupassant ever wrote—in French!—and they were tired of him. They admitted he was a clever beast, but wanted to hear something less beastly for a change. Something with a happier ending.

Well, I racked my mental stores, conning over Grimm's, the Decameron (yes, the naughty one), and Rabelais, rejecting them all as unsuitable either to my dignity or their tastes. I was not up to snuff on my Shakespeare, I fear. Finally, I bethought me of what was stocked nine inches deep on my sister's shelves, and lit upon Jane Austen.

Wary of floundering into a religious swamp or con-*trov*-versy, I selected *Mansfield Park* as the least likely to offend the sensibilities of my obliging driver or mar my already dubious reputation. It served to a treat, and the next fifteen miles went by most agreeably.

After I had concluded my recitative, we had to discuss the characters, of course, and I was invited to bed and board for the night. I accepted with thanks and gave the family a recap of *Persuasion* as my guest gift. They fed me like a prince of the realm: ham, pickles, fall tomatoes, biscuits with gravy, biscuits with butter, corn on the cob, a mess of greens and black-eyed peas that you couldn't nohow sneeze down the mountain, real coffee, more biscuits with jam, cheese with black walnuts, and an honest-to-God apple pie.

My luck held equally good, or the Goddess Fortuna smiled upon me (don't repeat that) for several more days. I was right glad, I must say, to have no more than a couple of hours on my feet for the first day, and a change of weather to make walking pleasant the rest of that week. I gradually inured my tender young muscles and slipshod spine to the effort of longer hours of walking, yet made excellent time down the road due to the kindness of my fellow creatures. Or perhaps it was simply greed in a non-material form—hunger rather.

Hunger for ideas and novelty, for up-country news and the chance to expound one's own views to a stranger. For I was obliged to listen a good deal. Not everyone attained to the level of taste of that French-reading farmer's folks. But there were plenty of folks happy just to hear my childhood impressions of life beside the sea.

I had only to describe the sight of ships in harbor, the smell of the sea, the solar lamp-lit night-fishing and crabbing expeditions, or repeat some of the sailors' naughtier jokes—to the men, anyhow. Every time I raised a snicker, I felt a surge of pride. Though uninitiated, I felt that I was beginning to be admitted to the confederacy of my sex; I was one inch closer to the men's mysteries.

For the ladies, I exgarbulated some poetry I had been obliged to memorize by the Grammarian; it was well received, I think. I hope they were not just being polite. Even in my youthful inexperience, I had found that ladies were apt to conceal their true thoughts, lest they hurt someone's feelings or prematurely reveal their counter-insurgent strategy. That's one thing you can say in favor of the Grammarian—you never stand in doubt of what she might be thinking.

On my fifth day toward, I was delighted to discover a stationery store that offered a mark-down on typewriter ribbons—a shipment had gone astray and there was no local custom for this type. Oh! What a find! Veni, vidi, emptori. I bought a whole boxful. The date on the box was only two years ago and it had never been opened. I learned from the box that the items were not made in Vermont, but in England—Old England, not New.

A bell of suspicion—with the sound of my grandmother's tongue for a clapper—rang in my head. Mislaid shipment, my foot! And other body parts, higher up. Oh what a riot there would be if I spent so much cash on a shoddy rip-off—or worse, a covert drug shipment, sealed up inside an innocent-looking box and 'accidentally' shipped to the 'wrong' address to be picked up later by someone wise to the drop.

Diffidently, I asked the proprietor—a nice motherly lady—if I might open the box before leaving just to make sure the contents of the box matched my sample. She had no objection at all, opened it herself and let me examine its contents. It was perfect—the exact item and one third the usual price. I had enough money left over to post the box back home with a saucy note and a handful of molasses candy to boot.

> *Hey! These were on sale, so I got them all. I'm taking one with me just in case the folks in Hitchins want to type up the hand-wrote pages themselves before permitting the September Volume to be included in the August Ranks of its Monographical Fellows. Seems a neighborly way to say how-do, don't it, Sissy? Pray do not scold me, Grandmama, for the ignorant-seeming sloppiness of my diction and vastly incorrect syntax. I am already reformed by the mere dread of incurring your disapprobation.*
>
> *Love to all,*
> *M.A.*

Having dispatched the package with a man known even in our way back holler to be a reliable Post Officer, I was feeling pretty exuberant. Only one quarter of the allotted minimum time and my mission was already one third complete! Neither the stationer nor the general store owner had shown more than polite interest—indeed, rather less—in my scheme of developing a new local market for re-inked ribbons. Sissy's ribbon samples went home with the new cartridges.

Five days of rather dusty trudging, eating exceedingly dry food from road caches, drinking from dubiously clean wells, and sleeping in barns or outbuildings tempered my enthusiasm for the wandering life. Suppers made of leavings grudged to me instead of the pigs, and the absence of routine bathing and laundering facilities—or worse, sullen looks from daughters tongue-lashed into providing me with these amenities in addition to their own heavy domestic duties—settled me right down into the dumps.

It was a bad patch for travellers, I tell you. Friends and relations! Each one ornerier than the last. Could enemies and strangers do much worse? I am convinced that one dearly revered daughter of the house would have cuffed me black and blue if she could get away with it. I was not so innocent that I had never received a smouldering look—but this one was of burning resentment and it was directed at my pretty clothes.

No rose pink hair ribbons for her. I would gladly have given mine to her had it not been sewn on to my britches as ornamental belt loops. She had her hair tied back with a narrow band of burlap. Her sack dress was the dullest dirty gray I ever saw outside of a nightmare. She may never have owned a scrap of color to wear, saving the scarlet of a split lip or the purple of an old bruise.

Soberly, I thought how Sissy might have fared in a household like this, and shuddered. Would she even have survived the scarlet fever? Stone deaf and not all that good-looking—what hope would she have of escaping her father's blows, or her husband's? For the first time in my life, I wished I were a girl so I could offer some help or comfort to this lonely, forlorn backwoods woman.

What welcome I might have received had I been tall, dark, rich, handsome, and less preciously pink in my attire is difficult to say: better from the ladies but worse from the daddies, I reckon. I was never less in charity with Mr. Darcy than on that stretch of road. He ought to have accepted the flattery, excellent service and good dinners with at least a modicum of good grace. I had to display the manners without benefit of the dinners.

Though no one says that Darcy is dark in coloring, I just picture him so. He may thank his lucky stars that he was fair of skin at least. I wondered if there had been many escapees from the tenant farms by people—men—wearing flounces and laces similar to mine.

If so, who made the frou-frou frockery for them? I had a whole raft of helpful females in my corner. Sissy received plenty of advice and aid from the Women's Sewing Circle at church. No one could doubt that these clothes were made *for me* and by a masterly hand. No wonder they say clothes make the man—rich raiment bespeaks a regiment of sisters and cousins and aunts—people of some numbers and substance—persons of high consequence in the country—not to be despised and not lightly to be crossed.

As I reached this conclusion, I began to think I had not given my sister near enough credit for her labors on my behalf. I might look to myself like a cross between a crepe myrtle and an explosion in a mattress factory—but to many others I might look like Little Lord Fauntleroy come to life—a ripe 'un, ready for plucking.

It was well for me that this thought sank in before I walked in, hot and thirsty, to a run-down quarter on the outskirts of Sumnerville. There was an inn standing temptingly nigh, with a porch that looked shady, if shabby. An uncovered, fly-haunted pitcher of gin-laced limeade stood on a table. I tell you I could smell the gin from the road. Maybe not from the open pitcher, as it seemed, but certainly wafting outward. Perhaps the wood walls were porous? Might the aroma come from the regular clientele, strewn casually about in rocking chairs and draped over the sagging porch rails?

My feet were sore, my back was aching, my whole corpus neglecti was hot, sweaty, and in no mood to make stipulations. The place looked good enough to me. My standards and spirits had been progressively lowered these past few days. But my lolling morale received a bracing boost from my honorable intentions to abide by my grandmother's fierce adjurations and strong prohibitions.

"Principles," she was apt to say, "are what give a man backbone. A man without principles is either an insect or a worm."

Now, I knew I had a backbone because mine was hurting like hell's own hop poles; nevertheless, I plodded past the attractively disreputable edifice. On the far side was revealed the stille nacht source of the fumes of 180 proof. If whiskey evaporation from sealed oaken barrels is the angels' share, Ye Olde Inn distillery must be distributing the fallen angels' share; juniper-laced mash fumes puffed lazily from the imperfectly sealed joints of its copper tubing. Tsk, tsk. Shiftless waste of good tincture foundation.

I trudged on another twenty or thirty minutes, into the town proper. There I sought the hospitality of a much cleaner and better kept way station. It happened to be run by people of color—exactly what color, I cannot say—there were Indians from India, Indians from west of Lumbeeland, Hispanics with a Cuban accent and some with a Maya cast of countenance, all conversing peaceably with the proprietors who were most likely of mixed Maasai and Joruba ancestry.

The instant I hove in sight with all sails and ruffles drooping, a child darted forth into the road with a dipper of spring water. I drank carefully, conserving enough of the dipper's contents to drizzle a trickle of water onto my snowy white linen handkerchief and wipe the dust from my face. The linen became less snowy and more slushy.

The boy came back twice more, once with a second dipper, then again with a full pitcher and a battered but clean aluminum tumbler. I drank and thanked and thanked and drank, and after my third tumbler's worth, my conscience smote me a sharp one upside the ear. Belatedly, I offered a dime to the little fellow.

He grinned and scampered off without pay saying, "Sarvice deed, sir Emissorry, y'all pass it on."

"I will, thank you. Where might I have a bath and a shave, friend?"

He pointed out the Bath-n-Barber and returned to his Welcome Post by the well.

The yard around the barber's place was hard packed dirt, swept clean. The porch was in apple-pie order. On a oilcloth covered table stood not one but three pitchers: one of pale, refreshingly sour raspberry beer, one of dark, aromatic root beer, and one of well water laced with thin slices of orange and lemon and a dab of salt and sugar. All three were covered with little squares of close-worked lace, weighted with beads—just like at home.

My dime bought me a glass of each, but I did not drink them right away. First, I had a welcome bath out back. Not a stingy shower: a real bath.

Cool water down the throat is hard to beat, but hot bath water does the trick. I felt so low and gritty that I was ready to rank cleanliness over godliness. No matter what it might do to my seized-up back muscles, I had been perfectly prepared to compromise every principle known to man in exchange for a brief cold water shower. But greater temptations were in store for me.

There, in all its seductive glory, was a copper boiler, reposing on its side, a la Madame Recamier: burnished mirror bright and cradled within a gleaming solar thermal mirror trough. This pleasing apparatus heated water smokelessly to a scalding 180 degrees Fahrenheit. I felt sure that M'sieur Louis Pasteur would have approved.

The coldwater tank or cistern was old and rusty in spots, but it had been patched in several places by proper welds, no lead solder to worry about there. Around each joint of the copper boiler's pipes, a leak-proof, food-safe sealant of bran, flour and salt kept in the steam—just like at home. I had to laugh. The unwashed moonshiners up the road could have learned a thing or two if they had ever condescended to take a town bath.

Hallelujah, praise be! Running taps allowed me to mix cold cistern with hot boiler water to a pleasant degree of tepidity, just above body heat. That bath felt mighty fine on my skin and twisty bones. After a good, long, soapy soak, I hopped out, kirtled a scarlet and turquoise towel about my waist, dunked my dust-defiled clothes in the used bath water, swished 'em about and shook them out. Hokey pokey for clothes, okey-dokey.

I was preparing to put them back on still wet — it would have been fine in that heat — when the lady of the household emerged and started fussing over them.

"I thankee, sar, for wrassling them duds out of the pre-rinse, you need not have troubled over that. I'll see to all that. Lordee! What a mess of ruffles you got there. Somebody love you a whole, whole lot. Now you git and sot yourself down in the chair and my man will shave you just the way you like."

I attempted to protest, but she ignored me. She turned a crank that upended the tub and sent the greywaters cascading into a filter bed surrounding the flower garden. She ran fresh hot water into the tub and got out the biggest laundry paddle I have ever seen in the hands of a woman. I, clutching my riotously colored towel about me, fled.

In the barber shop, I had two fellows ahead of me, but I was in no red hot hurry to stir my stumps. I savored my three-drinks-for-a-dime, starting with the beer and ending with the root beer. I had never had beer before, being underage and over religious. Casually sipping my first beer, lounging at my ease among my masculine peers, farther from home than I had ever been: I felt myself to be a man indeed. I snapped my metaphorical fingers at fussy female proscriptions.

Happily, the beer was not laced with anything stronger, and by the root beer I had reverted to a carefree boyhood. Lord-ee, that stuff was good.

By the time I was shaved (I fancied a new style with a thin line of mustachio and beard framing my chin—I thought I looked quite the dasher) mine hostess had those clothes soaped, rinsed twice, gently mangled, and the trousers pressed. She was deftly ironing every last curve of my ruffles with a specially made three-finger curling tongs. She displayed such marvelous skill and panache that I nearly applauded.

My vest was hanging up, ready for its turn. I rescued it from the hot iron (it had the coils of wire in it) saying gently, "Not that one—my sister says it will shrink and curl under the iron." I put on my clean, pressed trousers and wet vest, allowing it to cool me as it dried out.

She did not merely iron the ruffles, she actually *starched* them. When done, my shirt looked so much like an ice cream confection that I had to ask where I could find an ice cream parlour. She told me.

Yep, they had an ice house in a cave near the creek. And rock salt by the barrel.

Once I was fully dressed, I splurged on a hand-cranked dish of strawberry ice cream that matched my besplendant quasi-royal raiment in both color and curl. Altogether, I thought myself in high gig and so I was—for the time being. I supposed that my luck had turned again and I was going to be serenaded the rest of the way to New Destiny, floating on a gondola with a canopy and a platter of grapes.

It didn't turn out quite that way. Maybe that beer was stronger than I thought?

The prices of everything in town were so reasonable that I thought they must have been knocked down to encourage more Irregular Emissary trade. Later, I found out that was not the case. The prices were low because the whole town was a co-operative that shared profits, subscribed to the regional rail-road authority, and supported a mini-militia. This meant that they shipped their goods in and out, whole, entire, on-time, unspoiled, and untaxed by the protection racketeers that sailors call 'pirates' and other, less polite, names.

The way-stationers would not accept tips, so I made the lady of the house a present of one of my precious coils of copper wire. I was informed by all hands that they knew I was a gentleman born, and they offered me a ride part of the way onward by a lift on the slow barge going down. I felt I had taken enough advantage of their generosity and declined. I soon wished I had accepted. It would have saved me a lot of trouble.

It had previously been explained to me that alcoholic beverages in and of themselves were not evil. However their effects were unpredictable, and created conditions under which evil thrives. Sort of like mold is apt to eat books in a damp, humid corner of a library. A mere four ounces of lowrez beer was not enough to overset me, nor most people. But there were people whose reaction to alcohol was a black-out of their conscious mind and all the attendant evils thereof. They might run you down in a wagon or even shoot you dead—not only without conscious intention, but without any memory of the event. Conclusion? Know thy limits and avoid thine neighbors like yon plague.

Unknown to me, my conduct in by-passing the dubious hospitality of the Ramshackle Inn uproad had become a topic of discussion among the patrons thereof. They had but little to occupy the wide open spaces behind their noses on any given day; my advent provided free fodder for rumination and a handy target for condemnation—the role stray cats used to provide in London before the Great Fire. The trend of commentary on my appearance, intentions and family origin was almost universally unfavorable; however, opinions about my plumpness of pocket were decidedly optimistic.

The end result of this twin upwelling of error and furor was not to my immediate advantage. Of course, I knew nothing of the untoward notions of my fellow men until later. This intelligence was gathered by others, I merely report it here as a concurrent event to my own doings.

Some of the lounge-reptilia, having worked themselves up to a pitch of aggressive resentment decided to do something about me. A small contingent of activists, expressing a desire to "drown me like a kitten" betook themselves to their fishing boats, intending to find me down stream and carry out their professed agenda. They encountered a river patrol instead and were summarily bundled back to shore to sleep off their fume-induced bravery while tied to a tree.

The other party, less inebriated and more incensed, employed a superior strategy. They skirted the town, knowing full well that the border guards would turn them out as soon as they parked a toe one inch over the line. I may say that they knew this from experience. It was not a theoretical supposition. They were obliged to head south and go pretty far afield since the northern route was out of the question.

From Sumnerville, the nearest landing was about half a kilometer north of the main road. The town proper was situated on rising ground—a lesson learned from repeated flooding until the floating bamboo docks and mobile wheeled landing stages were jointly developed by Sumnerville and its sister towns on both sides of the river. After several incidents of daylight banditry, a system of tolls and changing checkpoints was established.

The river flowing north of the town formed a sort of defile between the levee and the bluffs: a narrow strip of land that was almost as easy to patrol as the river itself. One never knew exactly where the levy would meet the levee, so to speak. This scoundrel trap-works was likely to make my enemies' progress awkward, at best. Not to mention expensive and abortive should the riverfolk catch any whiff of their intentions.

There had already been certain passages of arms between these brave fellows and the river people on several occasions—mostly over poaching of fish weirs and illegal trapping. There was also some degree of general ill-feeling between the merchants who plied the river and the rowdier elements in the region.

The land to the south of the Trader's Trail was an impounded wetlands, constructed by the town as a haven for game and as a sewage treatment plantation. Humanure and green manure—comfrey chiefly—had been mutually reinforcing the soil there for some time. The land itself had once been infested with striga and was still unsuitable for grain crops. Over time, the gradual enrichment of the soil had suppressed the striga. The controlled and bounded flooding encouraged wild rice, reeds, wet-foot bamboo and over-wintering Canada geese to flourish.

It was rough, stinky going even for a bunch of whiskey-mad drunks. They passed easily through the open, park-like areas of coppicing southwest of town, then were forced to go farther south to avoid losing their boots in the bogland.

The territory just beyond the bog was copperhead country: a place where bootless man may boldly go just once. The barefoot do not tread into a nest of copperhead unless they want to wind up dead. End of story: enough said.

On the east side of town the town's collective canebrakes were thick; their berry patches were bramblier than hell's emergency hatch; their sunflower and flax fields were guarded by dogs bred for the purpose—a mix of collie, labrador, and rottweiler—who were not pleasant to encounter in person or in pack.

That is why it took the squad so long to circle back to the road to waylay me. It must have been a hot, tiring and thirst-raising journey. No wonder they were extra-irritated when they did catch me up. More than half of them had gotten disgusted with the chase, given up and gone back the short way, through the toll corridors, kept mowed, marked, and watched.

I am afraid I have no good clear recollections of my second encounter with the remaining party. For one thing, I did not see them at first. I was only warned by some second sight—a sense of menace such as a rabbit must feel when it is being stalked by an unseen hawk. Or a woman who is being eyed by a rapist. I do not remember what they said at first, or why I began drawing back from them. But I believe it was the way they smelled.

They stank like nothing else I have ever known—and remember, I have been around fish kills and seal-greased sailors. It wasn't the alcohol, either. They could not have been drunken still, sweating out the stuff for all the time it took to find me. Not unless they were carrying hooch with them the whole way.

But it was a sicker smell than mere booziness—like rot. I swear to you, there was something dead in that man already. Such dogged pursuit must have been motivated by more than ordinary malice. There was a quality of fanaticism in the one man's single-mindedness. I cannot account for it otherwise. I had done them no harm, unless to deny them my custom—they would not have been a dollar richer had I given it them. The only clue I have is a remnant of their verbal attacks on me, torn from memory and still ragged.

"... consorting with them shiftless *coloreds*." (He used a different term.) "You used to be waited on hand and foot, ain'tcha?"

"Yah, who does he think he is, anyway?"

"Too good to have a drink with his fellow white men."

"Reckon he must be a rich, fat-ass sucking son of a bitch—"

"Well, I do not know how you come to be acquainted with my grandmother—I suppose you must mean her, the description is so apt—but I assure you, good sirs, that we are none of us rich."

They did not know whether to laugh or sneer or turn up their toes. In the moment it took their brains to process the decision, mine took instant action. I ran like hell.

Clothing, designed to make one visible and hence less likely to be shot by mistake for a deer or squirrel, also makes it deuced difficult for one to hide in the woods. Alone, of course, one cares little for other's opinions. In town, one endures stares and opprobrious remarks with a shrug. A preux chevalier is accustomed to the envy of hoi polloi.

However, in the unwelcome company of a gang of drunken rowdies, about twice one's age and size, well, one tends to feel a trifle ridiculous. Not to mention terrified.

Leaping down hill in my starched, ruffly, fluffy garb, I soared, I sang through the air. I felt lighter than a cloud, a blown bit of blossom, a ragged scrap of foam torn from a whitecap by a furious gust of wind. Spindrift! That's me! Feeling so free!

It was as glorious a sensation as it was short-lived. The ape species Dolichopo-didae Rusticana had no trouble legging up to recapture me. One dumped out the contents of my day pouch and took the typewriter ribbon into his hand. I clutched the book pouch close to my body.

"What's this, little girly-man?" He took my wrist and tried to pry it up. I kept my armed folded close and a double grip on the book pouch. I used the trick of relaxed resistance: without straining, I simply held my arms and my grip in place. They struggled unsuccessfully to move my arms for about half a minute. Then the third fellow came up from behind.

"Break his little finger," he said.

Damn. He knows the counter trick.

Suddenly, there was a dark whoosh, two thunks and a sharp report. In that order.

The men who were holding my arms let go and dropped to the ground. Sounds of someone crashing through brush behind me. Another *pow* and a Doppler whine. I was still standing. My fuzzy vision—which I had suffered since I was eight—rapidly cleared to 110 percent sharp focus.

For a few seconds only, I had 20-10 vision. I looked down.

The man on my left had a gleaming, polished black arrow through his throat. Gagging horribly, he clutched at the shaft with his left hand. In his right, the mangled fragments of typewriter ribbon housing lay scattered on his open palm.

The guy on my right lay still and glassy-eyed. His arms were flung to either side. A little patch of bright red seeped out slowly, staining his snowy-white shirt. Was I in a fairy tale? I wondered. White as snow, red as blood, and black as ebony.

Then I realized I was in a murder mystery—probably the next victim. Without thinking, I flung my arms wide. The book I had been clutching tightly to my pink, frilly, ruffled chest I held out as far from me as I could get it without flinging it away.

I made no attempt to run. It would have been useless. I simply stood there, shaking, arms wide apart, waiting. Which would it be? Some cool part of me wondered, the arrow or the bullet? The Leaden Lady or the Feathered Tiger?

It was neither. The shot never came.

Death didn't come for me, but the death-dealers did. Two big-boned, bulky women emerged from the woods on my left—not the close thickets directly in front of me. My mental money was on those woods—that was where the shots had come from. The ladies now entering the clearing must be expendable—or rash.

I slewed my eyes towards them but made no other move.

As soon as they were within earshot I found myself saying over and over again,

"Don't hurt the book, please don't hurt the book, it's a good book, don't hurt it, please don't hurt it. It's worth a lot to you, please don't hurt it. It's an inter-library loan, really it is. It's valuable . . ." and so forth. Seemed like I could not stop talking.

Another part of me observed the curious fact that these women had dark green faces and green paste smeared on their hair and neck as well. That remote part of me wanted to ask why, but it could not get through the static of my fear that my mission would fail. I kept pleading for the safe passage of the book.

"Shaddup," said the smaller of the two women, but I couldn't, and babbled on. The big woman pushed me roughly, so that I staggered and almost fell.

"We know what to do with your kind," she said, unkindly. She raised a cloven ash handle with a stone ax twined into the cleft with rawhide. My observant self noted with mild interest that it was probably a ceremonial object of the Tengwhit clan. A scalper?

"Do you know, Dee, I sometimes wonder why I bother to train you." Instantly, the woman who had pushed me sprang away from my vicinity and pretended she had never been anywhere near.

The remark came from a tall, lean, dark-skinned blur who strolled out of the forest at a leisurely pace. When she came nearer, I could see a family resemblance between her and the woman who had ironed my shirt. She carried a longbow of impressive proportions.

Three more bow-women, a shot gunner and a riflewoman followed her. The five guardswomen looked around warily, keeping close watch on all directions. The tall archer directed her attention and her words to my would-be tormentor.

In a lazy drawl she said, "I think it must be because you have your somewhat limited uses."

Dee, caught bullying, looked like bullies usually do under such circumstances: she hung her head to one side, shamed, shook it in balked anger, and darted looks of mulish obstinacy towards her superior. As the archer continued, her voice hardened and sped up,

"But don't think I will put up with your insubordination forever. I have been patient because you were hurt as a child. But you know what? You are a warrior now, and under *my* command. So suck it up. If you keep on letting *your* feelings over-ride *my* orders I will decide you are not worth my trouble. You understand me?"

Dee mumbled some sort of assent.

"You all understand me?" said the archer, rounding on her troops, with a cold ferocity, "I expect to be obeyed even when I am not physically present. You see this asshead kind of behavior? *You* stop it! War is a sacred trust, not a place where you dump your girly shit. Got that?"

"Yes, ma'am," the replies came. "Yes, ma'am."

"If you are not here to protect the weak and aid the helpless then get away from me now. Before I decide to do something about it."

Nobody moved. I would have given her the odds, even against the Grammarian of Grandville County. Five to three, any time of day. Or night.

The archer turned her gaze on me. She held my eye for a long time—seemed like a long time, anyway. By this time I had managed to shut up. I just looked back at her.

"If you are a spy, you will not live to make your report."

I swallowed. I wanted to say "No, ma'am," with the firm intention of affirming the contrapositive to her insupportable assertion. But my voice got stuck on an "ah" somewhere down in my throat—a kind of a squeaky "ah" it was. Also, the lynchpin of my jaw appeared to have malfunctioned. So I just shook my head no, no, no. Several times, I believe.

"Why did you hold the book away from you?"

Now, this, I had an answer to. Simple, straightforward, no logical flip-flops required.

"Well, I thought—I thought I was next. And I saw the—the blood, you know. And I didn't want to get any of my blood on the book, maybe ruin it. It's an important book," I said earnestly, "It's worth a lot to you—if you get it to the Medsins. They'll pay you for it, honest! But it has to go to the Local Collections, My Grammarian said so, I—"

"What will they pay for you?" said the smaller woman who had come forward with Dee. I grinned, suddenly feeling an intense relief.

"For me? Nothing! The book is worth ten of me. A hundred of me! More!"

Then I laughed. And cried, and gasped and I don't know what all. I sank to my knees because I could not stand anymore. The archer looked down at me and made a decision.

"Hood him and bring him." A few more words, said rapidly—I think in a Tengwhit dialect—to the shotgun holder. The reply was too softly spoken for me to follow.

I was boosted to my feet. A bag fell over my head. It was secured with a cord around my neck, not tightly, but tight enough that it could not fall off nor be easily drawn off. It smelled of dust and someone else's sweat. Soon, it would be soaked with mine. I wondered who wore it last and whether he survived. That cold Something inside my head wondered who would wear it next and whether they would ask the same question about me.

A smooth, sanded stick was put into my hand and I grasped it. The other end, held by one of the Tengwhit, led off, tugging me along. Guided across changes in the ground by the dips and rises of the stick, I seldom stumbled. When I did, a heavy hand laid on my shoulder from behind steadied me. I suspect the hand was Dee's, and that she had been told off to escort me as her punishment for being willing to murder an unarmed man.

I thought that was also why Dee had been ticked off in front of me, in FTR English, rather than in her own language—to make the shame and blame stick harder to her hide. That was a good sign wasn't it? Or was it a trick to make me think I was safer than I really was? What if it was just to make a good story if the FTR delegation came to look for me after I was dead or tortured or some combination of the two?

I was thinking a good deal more rapidly than is my usual wont. Mentally, I kept adding up columns of Good Signs and Bad Signs. You may think of them as Positive Numbers and Negative Numbers. Unfortunately, I had so little real data that I might as well have been calculating with Imaginary Numbers.

Not dead yet—Good Sign. Not free to continue—Bad Sign. Book intact—Good. Book in hands of possible enemy—Bad, unless honorably delivered, in which case Good Enough, even if honorable Self not so Well Off. Escaped from thieves—Very Good. Escaped from potential beating or murder—Excellent. Prisoner of armed patrol—Not Good on the Whole, but considerably better than dead. Unless armed band had something in mind to make me *wish* I was dead—Much Worse than Plain Old Bad.

Oh, hell—this was worse than playing Sudoku. There were too many imponderables to impound in one pond. Punning was more my speed than cunning. I couldn't figure out what any of this meant.

Should I be thankful for my small stature and for being underage? Maybe they could not kill me outright because I was too young. Maybe they would just enslave me instead. Now there's a happy thought! Maybe I should just stop thinking altogether. If you can't think anything nice, then don't think at all. Better living through brainlessness.

I was a poor excuse for a scout, all right. A scout would know where they were taking him by the smell of the soil and scents of the trees. Not me, boy.

If I were not so short-sighted, I might have been a scout. But would they not have shot an obvious scout on sight? Of course, had I been a trained and cool-headed scout, I would not have been in this fix. Yes, but what about the obverse diagonally anti-contra-negative? If a scout *had* been in this fix, even he might not be cool-headed. Or have any good excuse. Or *something* like that. Logic was never my long suit.

After four or five days of slow marches—probably roundabout to confuse me, an unnecessary precaution in my case—we came to an interior village. On the way, I was only hooded, but at night my hands were also tied behind me and the cord around my hood secured to a tree. It was an uncomfortable way to rest; I got little sleep.

There was a slit in the bag just large enough for me to lap water from a bowl—like a captive animal—or receive nourishment. I chiefly ate beer and barley soup. Once I had a piece of dried tamarind leather. I chewed it a long time. It had little flavor except a bit of tartness on the tongue. I ate one meal per day, only when we halted for the night. I was never fed until after I was secured to my night tree.

When we finally came to our destination, I was put into a lockdown compound of wicker cages. My clothing, packs, band, and knife were taken away, everything but my determination was taken away. An interpreter came every day to ask what I wanted. I always told them what I wanted: to get the book safely to New Destiny.

Once, to vary the routine interrogation, I foolishly asked,

"Why do some of you ladies paint your faces green?"

"Why do you wish to know?"

"No reason. Just idle curiosity. Forgive the question."

No one would even think of looking for me until 60 days since I set forth. I had been chased off the Trail at day 11 or 12. I had been here a week or ten days. At the time, I strictly accounted for each day but I caught a feverish cold and lost track.

While I was feverish, I had vivid dreams, in which an extreme close-up view of the dead man's hand figured prominently. I saw the distinct patterns of his fingerprints, etched in dirt and fresh black ink. I could have drawn them to scale, taken the picture to the Sheriff's office and compared them, with complete confidence, to prints of any other felon on record. The lines of his palm, broken by scattered bits of typewriter ribbon housing, were curiously clear.

I saw that the ribbon advancing mechanism was deceptively simple. It was made of molded plastic, or resin. That could be mold cast in metal. Thin steel or maybe bronze. It would require a good deal of precision, but the whole thing could be redesigned, made with a pop-top or hinged access panel—in short, made easily reusable.

That part could be carved from heartwood, this cover plate made of floated glass, perhaps, or thin-shaved horn. Translucent seashell, maybe. Hmm. . . . And the ribbon itself, tensioned with little springs and advanced by what looked like a cam or half-gear . . . yes. . . .

I would *never* have dared—never have *dared* to break open a ribbon cartridge and examine its innards. But he had done it for me. Poor fellow.

I know, I know—he was a bully, the very type and mold of bullies, the sort of person I had hated all my life, yet he did me a huge favor. And paid for it with his life. It was my weakness, my cowardly running away that had cost him everything. His sacrifice had given me tremendous hope and purpose, a path to my future and the rights of manhood.

When this dream was uppermost, I sobbed and trembled and pleaded for forgiveness. I freely acknowledged my debt and the sacrifices made for me. I humbly and truly thanked everyone for their help. When I was awake, I was glad, glad, GLAD the three were dead.

Awake, I felt a rush of pride that I had led those cut-throats, however unwitting, into deadly danger. Had they not intended for me a death or a humiliation worse than death? If I were to fail in this one simple mission, I might never gain my manhood. The damnable cowards. Three to one! Against me! Oh! I was in high glee that they should be dead and I still alive. The only hitch in my happiness was that mine had not been the hand to cut them down to size. Had I killed them myself, I would be a man indeed!

In another dream I was always going up-mountain, jauntily. My back was straight and I was a lot taller. I faithfully executed all my other commissions, except for the typewriter ribbon. I couldn't seem to get over it: the sight of that fellow lying flat, staring into eternity with an arrow in his throat and the bits of typewriter ribbon housing strewn across his palm. I was soundly and furiously berated for it, but I refused to be bullied. After all, I was a man. A man does not respond to un-merited and sneering remarks: that is a boy's trick. In this happy dream, a winter trader out of Vermont brought us some brand new ribbons—made in England, no less. My lapse was forgiven, or at least mercifully forgotten.

But both moods changed when a third dream gained strength. In this dream, I felt nothing, nothing at all: neither sorrow nor pity nor pride; neither guilty gratitude nor schadenfreude. No victorious triumph, no pride of achievement. I was secure in my heart that I had done all I could to fulfill my mission and no man can do more than his best.

Three men were dead on my account. That was so. And so what? It had no meaning. All men must die. They died in dishonor, while I yet lived, honor intact (so far). Their death was not my fault. They had no business interfering with my duty and breaking sacred laws. Perhaps it was a pity that my manhood mission was marred by another man's death; perhaps it was only just. The fulfillment of my duty yet lay before me; there was no occasion to be puffed up. When the mission was complete, then I could walk in a man's shoes. Not before.

This was a comforting thought. The only problem with this dream was that in it, my grandmother said that I was not to blame. Oh, really? Since when?

I distrusted my dream and myself. I had never experienced the least jolt of spiritual revelation in my year and a half of residence in my grandmother's . . . well, cult. My folks had escaped to the northeast and gone to sea just to get away from that bunch of people. How would they feel if they knew that I sang hymns to my-self and found comfort in them in my cage? I burrowed into the straw like any wee mousie. Was I a rational man or an animal?

"You are a MAN-imal," my dead mother assured me. "Grrrrraaar!" She attacked me with a fierce stuffed animal, making me giggle as I used to do at bedtime, lying immobile in my cage of straps and bamboo braces. My dead father stood on the deck of a sloop in a pelting sideways rain, singing a hymn he learned in childhood. He looked at me and smiled. It was a smile compounded of shame, resolution, sadness, and what I can only call complicit humor.

"We're in the same boat," he said. "Keep your weather legs on. Walking on water. Buoy dead ahead. Shoal 'nuff!"

When that dream faded, I was no longer worried about my fate, or the fate of the book. I regretted not getting some word back to Sissy, but doubtless all she needed to know would eventually reach her—one way or another. I slept soundly for the next few nights.

Some time later, I was brought before a council of judgment composed of seven elders and two generals. The elders wore imposing robes of silk dyed in vivid solid colors: red, white, green, black, blue, yellow, purple-crimson. The generals were clad in brown and green forest camo. I wore my old linen underthings and my trousers.

The tale of my being chased, captured, and questioned were rapidly communicated to them in Tengwhit argot. My well-ruched road clothes and woven silk identity band were fingered and murmured over. My one question about the green faces was also mentioned. I only know this because a rough translation was given to me by a young interpreter, scarcely older than a girl.

"What do you know of herbs?"

"Not much. I am no doctor. I am only a poor relative of the Medsin clan."

A small earthenware pot of the green paste was handed to me. I smelled it and tasted it. I smeared a small dot onto my forearm, where mosquitoes had been feeding freely on my blood. The ointment was soothing. Mosquitoes avoided it.

"Pennyroyal?" I ventured. "My sister uses it sometimes. I know where to gather it but not how to use it. Does it help the complexion?"

There was laughter as my question was translated. My judges seemed to relax and I thought that they might actually do what I ask, deliver the book for me. I did not think I would ever leave that place, alive or dead. But if the book was sent on, with my identity band, my name would be remembered and I would die a man, not a boy.

"We will examine the book."

"Please do."

All of them handled the book—smelled it, rubbed spit on it, held a handwritten page over a lit candle. I trembled during this test and Dee looked gleefully at me.

"Aha! You fear that your secret writing will be exposed!"

With as much dignity as I could command, I answered, "There is no secret writing. I fear for the safety of the book. The only secret is in the writing itself—it tells how to cure spine fever with herbs."

"Could be in code," said the black-robed judge, frowning over the pages and throwing a dubious glance at me.

"True," said the archer. "But if he's clever enough to code maps or porn into a volume of herbal biochemistry we ought to hire him as an intelligence officer. Think of all the secret messages we could send!"

I expected a show of temper, but Black Robe simply made a moue, raised a languid eyebrow and gave a half nod of assent. She passed the volume over to Red Robe with no other comment. She seemed unconcerned and not in the least put out.

From somewhere—possibly my calm inner observer—I gathered a notion that Black Robe was accustomed to having her ideas discounted and did not care one way or the other. It was her task to find fault, so she found fault, without tainting her ideas with rancor or prejudice. She reminded me—inversely—of the Grammarian.

I wondered if I would ever see the Grammarian alive again. How she used to rant about the people I was to take the book to.

"Now, you, Marcus Aurelius, you listen to me. You take that book to one place only: the Local Collections office. You hear me?"

"Yes, ma'am."

"Nowhere else. Nobody else."

"No, ma'am."

"You think you know better than me and try to give that to the doctor chaps, they'll show you the door and put a boot upside your butt to help you through it. Think they are the world's own royalty, they do . . ."

And off she would go, muttering fiery imprecations and dire threats. Reminiscing, I unconsciously smiled.

"Prisoner, why do you smile?"

"I am sorry, your honors. My attention wandered. I was thinking of our Grammarian, who is also my grandmother. Of the things she says. She would 'send dogs to chew on my liver' if she knew where I was now—and how I am failing to carry out my mission. If I do bring shame on my people," I said proudly, "it is no fault of my forebears. Let the records show: I was well taught."

I stood stiff and straight. I might have a curvaceous spine, but it was still a backbone!

No matter what happened to me, I still had—however slim—a chance to complete my mission. If I could only convince my judges of the truth, there was still a chance.

Short of sight, short of stature, I might be, but by Goddess! I was more of a man than those thieves ever were! I was more of a man than I even knew myself. Did I not walk alone, half sighted and half height, yet have the courage to resist them?

They swaggered and strutted and thought themselves big men, but they were as small and twisted in soul as I was in body. Had they ever in their lives had the strength to say those three little words: I am sorry?

"The fault was entirely mine. I was pursued by thieves. I feared and I ran. I apologize for violating territorial bounds. I had no wish to trespass; I have no fear of your penalty. I am ready and willing to abide by your law. I ask only that this book be brought safe to New Destiny Library Local Collections. That is my Chief's mission and the only one of merit. If I succeed in this, my life is yours to do as you will. If I fail in this, none will mourn me. Only the loss of the book—the knowledge in it and the labor of making it."

My long speech was translated by a more expert communicator. The Elders conferred, bending their heads together and speaking in their own tongue.

Judgment was passed on me in both languages.

"You must be lashed for daring to walk on the Way—even though you were ignorant and are weak-eyed. For you brought others with you, less honest and more soul-faulty."

I bowed.

"And the book?"

"That remains to be decided."

I took my lashing and was returned to my cage. It was not too bad. The cuts were shallow and a calendula ointment was put on them by my captors—an unexpected mercy. The weather turned wet and cold. A tarp was thrown over the corner of the cage where my straw bedding lay and a rough blanket was added to my comforts. For the next few days I received slightly better food.

I retained my trousers and was also given back my socks to wear at night. I kept them clean and dry as I could. Once the cuts no longer bled freely when washed, my captors gave me back my shirt, vest, and identity band. The book, my knife, my shoes, my fire starters, everything else they kept. But they also gave me back my freedom.

I was escorted all the way south by scouts and small detachments of hunter-warriors along paths kept secret and seldom trod by men. In fact, I didn't tread on them either. I was carried most of the way, strapped to a litter. I felt like an overgrown papoose. Or, let us be more dignified, like an accident victim. A kind of non-ambulatory ambulance.

Once or twice a day I was unhitched from my flat prison to do that which no one can do for me. My guards never left me alone to do my business in the bushes, but, thanks to my previous medical experience, I was neither shy nor sensitive on this point. Besides, I was too happy in the opportunity to flex my limbs to care.

Long stretches of the trip took place by water. In wider waters I rode in large cargo skiffs; through narrower channels I went by low-riding hollow log canoes. These canoes had been fire-hollowed and still smelled slightly burnt. The lighter, shallower craft were stabilized and made more buoyant with reed-bundle outrigging.

Secured to my litter by straps and blankets, I often lay in the bottom of the canoes. My straight dead weight actually added ballast and diminished the tendency to roll, pitch, and yaw. Only my limbs were bound; my head was free to turn side to side. It was no worse than time spent in my bamboo treatment cage, and no better.

Instead of my sister reading Grimm's to me while I lay immobilized, I was able to watch the clouds moving overhead in great misty blocks of color. I heard many birds on either shore. I imagined I could understand their language, like the fellow in the fairy tale. I told myself stories about this or that hero's journey.

Once, I made the mistake of comparing my peculiar mode of present day progress to those of ancient epic, story, and song. Some hero, me! Crafty Odysseus, swaddled to poles in the bottom of a reed boat. Well, I had to laugh—silently of course. In fact, I laughed so hard that I shook the canoe, causing water to slosh in over the low-riding gunwales and settle beneath me. That effectively sobered me down. New motto for modern travellers: when the futtock is next to the buttock, and the craft is made of chaff, don't laugh.

In larger craft I was balanced across the thwarts, slightly above the bilge. For the journey away from the village of judgment I was hoodwinked again; but after that, I was largely allowed to see whatever there was to see. A lot of what I saw was sky. The sides of a canoe can only hold my interest for a limited amount of time.

Oh, no, I mistake: there were a couple of portaging passages I was not permitted to see. For those, my eyes were covered. They needn't have bothered; I could not have identified any but the most massive landmarks. But, there I was: a kind of third canoe to be portaged, but slightly less useful. And there were sacred sites where I was not even allowed to enter. They had to carry me all the way around over very rough ground. Fortunately, however supine I might have been, I was not prone to seasickness.

The hood was removed, just before we took to the river again. For my toilet break, I was released from the cloth webbing that held me to the litter by the women who had carried me. They were shorter than me, but by no means smaller. Both litter bearers were extremely short, fat, narrow-shouldered and unbelievably muscular.

They patted me all over, grinning and reaching for my red hair. I bent down to let them see my scalp at nose level. They smelled of beer breath and bear grease. Once they were satisfied that my hair was natural, not dyed nor a wig, they laughed and chattered to one another. Without warning, one of them seized me by the waist and boosted me up over her head, apparently to show off how strong she was. The other one laughed.

She held me sideways, with one hand under my back and the other under one thigh. I stayed relaxed, though my first instinct was to tense up. Aloud, I spoke their word for "down" and added a "please" in the Tengwhit language. I swore something awful in sign language, though. My sister's reading tastes had made me fluent in silent cursing. Great stuff in Shakespeare, Tristram Shandy, and Rabelais.

The Tengwhit leader looked around and rattled off something in Bearer lingo. Her tone of voice was gruff with an underlying note of amusement. So they put me down, patted me again, smiled with surprisingly white teeth, and vanished, singing, into the undergrowth beneath some tall sweetgums and sycamores.

I was prevented from stepping into the boat by the scout.

"So you are a spy, after all."

"No, ma'am."

"What then were you saying with your hands?"

She had a perfect visual memory. She repeated back to me with flawless accuracy everything I had said in the air, including words my sister and I had made up. I translated for her. She still did not trust me until we came to the next village—not until she confirmed my translations with the folk at the Moravian school for the deaf. Some of my more shocking expressions were taken up by a group of giggling boys. Somewhere, sometime, somehow—among a nice, polite group of people there will be one kid who goes off into the blue, swearing like a Shandian sailor.

For this lapse in good judgment, I was again strapped into my litter instead of being allowed to sit up like a regular passenger. Oh, well. Patience is also an heroic virtue. It was good for me, I guess. I did my isometrics for hours at a time.

For the last leg of the journey, we took passage on a larger craft, some variety of cargo skiff. Since we were travelling on waters that were open to all, not those kept for women only, they lowered my feet, tilting me so that I could look around better. Around the lakes I saw some beautiful, if blurry, countryside. The leaves were changing.

I was de-littered well before we came in sight the Medical Center in New Destiny. I dare not imagine what would have become of me had I been carried through those gates on a stretcher. I would probably be there now, still undergoing tests. Happily, however, I walked in on my own two feet, like a proper hero, and dressed accordingly.

All of my belongings were restored to me intact. Including the book. I tried to give my hard-working escorts three of my precious coils of copper wire, but they would not take them—they seemed slightly insulted that I should offer.

"We take no pay for guarding you. You have walked upon no Trader's Trail." A note of pride rang in her voice. "This is the Women's Way."

I bowed, deeply as I could with a stiff, scarred back.

A comedy of errors ensued when I arrived at the Library Complex. Instead of being shown to the librarians' quarters, as requested, I was led to the baths. I probably needed one. There, the lashing I had received was discovered. It excited a great deal too much concern. So did the state of my spine, which was alarmingly clucked over.

I was not permitted to go anywhere I chose until the cuts had been treated. Retreated, that is. I restrained my impatience and kept a taut thong on my tongue. I knew not what dangers nor intrigues might yet occur to thwart the completion of my mission.

I was sent to doctor after doctor, all conversing literally over my head (but not above my comprehension) about my spine and what could be done for me. Swimming and stretching were most often recommended, but one woman insisted that I be seen by a certain yoga master. This was done. I was instructed for a solid hour in new exercises and finally released on my own recognizance. (By the way, the exercises did help.)

Then my poor eyesight was discovered. Another long examination. Finally, someone remembered their guest manners and offered me a meal. By now, I was too ravenous to decline. I ate a bit wolfishly, I am afraid. Even so, I kept a leash on my appetite lest someone suspect me of harboring a tapeworm and subject me to another series of tests.

Throughout all, I kept a grip on my bookbag and allowed no one—*no one*—to take it from my hands. Thankfully, post-traumatic stress was not suspected as the root of my obsession. They have *ways* of dealing with PTSD at New Destiny.

Instead, I was laughed at for a fool and a bumpkin; my pride suffered worse from the tongue-lash of urban insults than my back did from a light and essentially just flogging. But, by Odysseus, I held onto my book.

Late that afternoon, just before the library closed for the night, I reached the book's destination. Impressive, those hallways: the cool stone walls guarding so many volumes; the swift, thin-bladed fans, running on bi-metallic current; the mist-covered steel pipes, cooled by icy waters from the labs, sucking moisture out of the humid air and drip-watering the plants in the windowboxes; the great masonry stoves like squat, brick giants, captured by mystic spells, kept asleep all summer, but waking to red life in winter, sworn to the Service of the Books to keep them dry and warm.

The Local Collections librarian was seated in a tiny office at the base of a well of books. The shelves went up at least ten yards, I joke not. A couple of planks on pulleys supported the aerial acrobats who acted as book finders. They had already descended for the day and were bidding farewell to the librarian when I came in. I handed her the book that had cost me some pains to deliver.

"This is a work of medicine," she said, glancing at the title and flipping through the pages with maddening casualness. "You should take it to the medical facility."

"No, my Grammarian said to bring it to you."

"To me?" She looked bewildered.

"To the Local Collections. That is you, isn't it?"

"Yes. But why me?"

"I do not know."

"Who is your Grammarian?"

I told her. She sat very still for a moment, then she smiled.

"Oh," she said. She put out her hand for the book. I gave it to her. I stood there a moment longer, looking uncertain. She smiled.

"Don't worry. I'll see that it gets to the right people."

She gave me a stamped metal dog tag receipt for the volume. I tucked it carefully away in the lining slots where my coils of copper wire still were.

My mission was complete—at least the down mountain part. I lucked out on the up-mountain trip. The yoga master's apprentice latched onto my case like a leech. He was going on his internship/journeyman's journey to treat people in the back of beyond. As a Medsin clan relation on my mother's side, I was entitled to claim a course of treatment for my condition. My enthusiastic yogic guardian would scarcely let me out of his obsessive compulsive sight. So I got to ride on the Alco-operative boats after all.

Me and a pair of corrective lenses. For the first time in my life I saw clearly the leaves of trees. I thought, *You know, I could get used to this.* I do not know to this day who paid for my first eyeglasses; but ever since then I have paid with my own earnings. They were cheap, set into a bamboo frame, not tortoise shell and resin. But they meant I could see where I was going—in more ways than one.

Lock after lock, we rose up the rivers in fine rainy weather. Loch after loch we sailed; or were dragged along canals by wet mule teams. I did my exercises; Doc Berry Yogic (a pseudonym) took measurements of my slowly shifting, un-drifting spine every day and wrote up case notes by night. I have never seen anyone so completely happy in their line of work. It was frightening. I wished I had a clove of garlic or a silver cross about my person. Just kidding.

Whenever the boatmen tried to frighten and buffalo us about what was happening on the waters, I gave them a taste of Old Norfolk grogg-noddy to put them firmly in their place. I rattled off ever so much bilge about praams, proas, funnys, feluccas, and fryboats to keep them quiet.

Then I loftily turned to discussions with the Doc about the combinatorial synergies of moon-harvested extractions and the correct courses of therapeutic sequencing for herbal tinctures. They called me "the little Professor", and I tolerantly dubbed them "lake-lubbers".

Honorable combat having been joined on these terms, I tried my best to scare the bejeezus out of the boatmen with tales of horror from the crypts of cholera or by detecting in them the dread signs of yellow Nile fever, but the Doc kept spoiling my act with soothing reassurances. So I read the books I was bringing home instead.

For my sister, I had brought back two books by the same author, both recommended as being funny. They were a smashing success. One was *Eggs, Beans, and Crumpets*. I forget the title of the other one, but I remember one of the incidents in it. When Florence Cray discovers that Bertie has stuffed his top hat with pages torn out of her novel *Spindrift*, shouts of laughter came out of my sister's room. She choked and sputtered. I went in to whop her on the back and dislodge whatever she had swallowed in her mirth.

"Ow, ow," she signed, wriggling away. "How would you like it if I did that to you?"

"I'd have to suck it up," I told her, and showed her my scars. I wouldn't let her or my spiritual aunts fuss over me, though. I just made them sit down and listen to my new plan.

"I'm going to 'prentice with the watchmakers in Dermton," I said. "In Destiny they say everyone at the watchmakers' is shortsighted—it's an advantage in the Trade."

Oh, there was a good deal more fuss, but I made my decision stick. Because I'm a man, now. I completed my manhood mission and I've served my people well. I get to choose my own path from now on. Don't talk to me about wiresmithing, we already have wiresmiths galore. Not me. I'm going to Dermton and maybe as far as Vermont.

Maybe England.

I'm going to earn hours as a precision lens grinder until I can apprentice to a Medsin watchsmith. I'm going to learn how to fashion tiny springs and thin metal flanges. I'm going to build up my toolset of delicate precision instruments. And then I'm going to come home and set myself up in business making typewriter ribbons.

Because there's a lot of good writers up there in the hollers. People with things to say that are worth saying. Speaking for myself, I think that fellow—what's his name?—may be wrong. Just a teensy bit wrong. Maybe—if you don't set yourself up too high—or knock yourself down too low—expect too much—demand too little—maybe you can go home again.

One other thing: I had not forgotten my acquaintance from hell's forecourt. What white knight fails to aid a captive lady? I did what I could. On my trip upriver, for the passage between Windrock and Bear Mountain I engaged myself to read aloud to an old lady for an hour each day. She liked my Norfolk accent and complimented me on my pronunciation. I earned enough cash to buy a few bright hair ribbons and sateen roses.

I forged a round-hand note from Sissy and signed her name. The note thanked the young woman for taking care of her little brother. I posted this gift from the stationer's shop, directing to my late acquaintance. I hope she was allowed to receive it; but if not, I hope she escapes.

You see, I also had told Dee of the Tengwhit about the young lady's situation, and asked her and her mates to pay a social call. After dark, perhaps? There's more than one way to skin a skunk: preferably by proxy. We cannot all be knights with a long lance and a white charger. Some of us have to be the generals. The Grammarian taught me that.

The Yoga Doc is coming back for me in the spring.

One more winter, and then I'm out of here. I can hardly wait. Meanwhile, I keep doing my exercises, reading maps and dreaming. Daydreaming, I mean. My nightmares have all been put out to pasture.

The Grammarian doesn't say much, but I believe she is secretly proud of me. Having at least one of her brood chicks accepted into a Medsin nest gives her a remote degree of self-satisfaction. Or maybe she thinks inflicting me on them is a form of just vengeance.

Sissy won't miss me. She'll be getting hitched this summer, I reckon. She has two men already promised to her as co-husbands. One of them is building her a house and the other one is turning the furniture for it. Between them, there's hardly a tree in the holler that doesn't shriek with fear when Sissy's suitors look at it. Fortunately, Sissy is deaf as a post and she can't hear the awful sounds they make. The trees, I mean, not the husbands.

But I'm going to miss this place, I reckon. When I'm deep down in the hot, drear, humid flatlands, fussing for seven solid years over glass dust or broken chronometers, I will miss the mountains. I'm sure I will. The cedars, spruces, and pines. Not just one or two individuals, seen close up, but the whole, wide range.

I can see it all so clearly. Deer poised on the ridge. Rabbit tracks. Deeply forested winter mountainsides. Beauty enough to make a man's heart ache. Right now, the valley looks like a fairy tale come true: white with snow; red with holly; and the tall, slender, arrow-straight trunks—gleaming wet, and black as ebony.

NIGHT BIRDS ON THE ROOF OF THE WORLD

BY LAWRENCE BUENTELLO

The dog still hadn't found any water by the time the Uncle decided they must stop. Keira was too ill to travel any longer.

Keira was Tam's age. She had fallen sick a week earlier, though she had still been strong enough to begin the journey. Tam liked Keira very much, because everyone else was older, and tended not to play with him—at least, not willingly. The two older boys, the brothers Brin and Brody, now lowered the crossbar of the hand cart on which they pulled the clay jars of water, blankets, and implements that would help them build a new place to live, should they find one. Keira also lay in the bed of the cart, curled into herself like a small, cold animal. The brothers stood listening to the Uncle, who gazed down on Keira as he shook his head sadly. He leaned on his walking staff and motioned toward a small collection of ruins at the foot of a nearby hill.

Behind the cart, walking slowly, and only stopping when they came near, was the ugly girl, Lauren, and the old blind man. She was only ugly because of the wounds on her face, but she was kind, and treated Tam sweetly. The old blind man, as thin as a willow switch, was full of stories, delightful stories that Tam always enjoyed. Tam was sad for Keira, but also filled with a secret joy, because he knew the old blind man might tell them a story tonight. He loved hearing the old man's stories; his words filled Tam with wonder and excitement. The old man always spoke of exotic and beautiful things.

The Uncle, a sinewy man of high morals who Tam obeyed like a father, whistled sharply to the dog, which raised its dirty white head and then hurried to the Uncle's side. Tam knew the only reason the Uncle kept the dog was because it was so good at finding water. Once, too, when something very large and frightening stalked them from the darkness just beyond the firelight of their camp, the dog paced and growled and kept the beast at bay.

Now the Uncle slapped the side of his leg and the dog followed alongside. He motioned to the brothers to pull the cart toward the ruins. Tam, Lauren, and the old blind man followed behind. The sun was falling low in the sky; Tam knew it would soon be evening. He imagined sitting by the fire, having a cool drink of water, and hearing a new story from the old blind man, something wonderful, something magical.

After the brothers pulled the cart to the ruins, and the Uncle had cleared a space in the weeds, stones, and debris beyond the first tumbled wall, Lauren wrapped Keira in several blankets, carried her from the cart, and placed her on the ground inside the clearing.

Tam sat next to the girl, touching her hand occasionally to let her know he was watching over her, while the Uncle guided the old blind man to sit on a large stone. In a moment, the brothers brought the jars of water into the cleared space for safekeeping.

The Uncle knelt by Keira, patting Tam on the back and smiling as he did so. Then he gazed at the girl seriously.

"Will she be all right?" Tam asked.

The Uncle brushed the back of his hand against Keira's cheek, then patted her hair gently. "She has a fever," he said, but not with any inflection Tam could judge as hopeful or fearful. "I pray she'll recover."

"I'll pray, too," Tam said, though he only closed his eyes for a moment, because he had no repertoire of prayers to consult. When Tam opened his eyes again the Uncle had gone, so he sat quietly for a few minutes staring at his friend and hoping she would be well again.

The brothers and the ugly girl took turns moving in and out of the circle and dropping kindling for a fire onto the dirt. The Uncle built a ring of stones for the fire, and then everything was done as it should have been, in preparation for the night.

As the others fussed over the construction of the fire ring, Tam rose and wandered to the edge of the ruins.

He stared down the winding dirt path along which they had traveled, sighing at the desolation. They had passed several hills, which glowed with red and golden hues as the setting sun cast dying rays against their rocks. Turning, he gazed along the length of the path they had yet to travel, as dry and desolate as the place from which they had come. But the sun blinded him to the details of the land beyond the ruins, so perhaps there was something more to see, some place that bore a gentler landscape. He remembered seeing fruit trees when he was very young, which died in the place the people had settled in those days.

There were many more people then, but now it was just him and Keira, the brothers, the ugly girl, the old blind man, and the Uncle. Tam remembered other places, but not very well, because they hadn't stayed in these places for very long. Something evil always pursued them, whether wild beasts, or depraved men, or phantasms of a nature he couldn't imagine.

He felt something brush his leg and stared down, startled, but it was only the dog. The dog gazed up at him as if to ask a question, but it was only a dog, and Tam had no idea what a dog might be thinking, if anything. The dog would not still be with them if it wasn't for the water it found. The dog had a gift, the Uncle once said.

Tam became aware of the hunger in his stomach, rising like acid in his throat. Perhaps if the dog had one gift it might have others, and if it could read his thoughts then it would know that he was thinking of other dogs the people had found, and what had happened to them. The dog watched him carefully.

But perhaps the Uncle had sent the dog to fetch him, and since he was weary of staring at the desolate land he turned and walked back into the ruins.

The dog followed, then lay down by the first wall, watching the sky and occasionally sniffing the air.

Tam sat by Keira again, and thought she seemed very fragile, so he invented a prayer and whispered it under his breath.

That evening the fire rose up in the ruins like a bright lantern against the shadows of the night. The Uncle had built a worthy fire ring, against which the embers caromed ineffectually.

After taking his water, Tam sat by Keira as the Uncle lifted her head and tried to pour a few drops into her mouth. She sputtered, but didn't seem able to swallow. The Uncle wet her lips and lay her on the blankets again, sighing. When he left to return the jar, Tam crept closer to the girl and studied her pale face in the light; he called her name, but she didn't respond. Only days before they had been playing together, throwing stones at the lizards that fled the brightening sun.

"Don't be sad," Lauren said as she kneeled by Tam.

Tam glanced up at her, and she reflexively pulled her scarf over her scars. Tam didn't even notice the scars anymore, but Lauren always seemed to know when someone's gaze fell on them, and she always reacted the same way.

"Will she be all right?" Tam asked.

"I don't know," Lauren said, touching Keira's cheek as if to sense the depth of her illness. "She's very sick."

"Will she die?"

"She's very young," Lauren said in the way of a reply. "She's very young, and she's very sick."

Tam didn't want Keira to die. He wished he knew how to make a good medicine, but the Uncle had given her the best medicine he could distill from the plants available on their journey, and she still hadn't gotten better.

"Perhaps we'll know in the morning," Lauren said as she rose and walked toward the shadows, one hand bringing the corner of her scarf to her eyes.

Brin and Brody knelt by Keira for a moment, but they said nothing to Tam. He could only wonder what they were thinking, but they never said much and always seemed sad. They had dirty faces, and large, brown eyes, and their prominent cheekbones and sunburned skin gave their heads the appearance of leathery skulls. When they found pretty stones they would give them to the children, so Tam knew they were kind, very kind, but very sad.

They rose away from Keira, though Brin touched Tam's hair as he passed, gently.

Later, when the night was deep and the darkness absolute, they all sat by the fire, and the Uncle turned toward the old blind man and said, "Tell us a story, Old Father, before we sleep."

Tam's eyes widened. He felt his heartbeat throb in his chest, for he'd been waiting all evening for the old man to speak. It wasn't proper for him to ask the old man himself, so he had to wait for the Uncle to ask, if the Uncle decided to ask at all; but now the excitement rose up in his chest, casting away the sadness he kept for Keira.

The old blind man's eyes glimmered whitely in the firelight. He braced his cheek against his walking stick, his face skeletal in the yellow light of the flames. "Would everyone like to hear a story?"

Tam waited for the others to speak before he joined in with an emphatic, "Yes!" The old man smiled toothlessly, enjoying the small acclaim he found in the group, and nodded.

Tam remembered some of the other stories the old blind man told them—stories of oceans full of strange, giant animals swimming in the water and talking to one another in a secret language; of the fantastic machines that flew through the sky with people inside of them, sweeping through the clouds and traveling all over the world; of the grand farms and the fertile deltas where great tribes of people lived together in a land of plenty; of the mythical creatures of ages past, winged lions, fire-breathing serpents, and gold-clad giants in desert lands bearing the heads of dogs and cats.

Tam lay in the dirt by Keira, pulling the corner of one of her blankets under his head, and listened intently to the old man's voice—grave, and rich, and shattered by the years.

That night the old blind man told a story Tam had never heard before—of the night birds that perched on the roof of the world, so huge that six men standing shoulder to shoulder couldn't compare to the breadth of a single bird's wing, nor could any axe hewn from the densest granite match the strength and power of a single bird's beak. These were the birds of the gods, and they nested in the eaves of the celestial frame that held the stars above the earth. At times the birds could be seen flying above the clouds, eclipsing the moon as they flew up to sharpen their beaks on the pure white lunar stone. But they were not just beautiful decorations for the gods, they were also godly emissaries. They collected precious manna from the secret places of the earth, and stored it in their nests; and when someone called up to the stars in the quiet of the night, begging for a morsel to eat, the birds would hear that person's cry, and if he or she was sincere, if he or she was a good, pious person, one of the birds would fill its beak with manna, spread its colossal wings and drift down to deliver this divine gift to the hungry person calling—

What a beautiful story! Tam thought, as he fought to keep his eyes open. Sleep crept from the night into his head, making him drowsy, but he didn't want to sleep; he wanted to hear more.

The old blind man may have said more, but Tam's eyes lost their battle against his weariness, and he finally closed them and lost the world, though the night birds returned in his dreams.

Tam woke in the early hours of the morning, while the night still threw its net of darkness on the world. He sat up, blinking his eyes at the smoldering embers of the dying fire. In the spare light he saw the others lying on the ground asleep. He looked toward Keira, but she lay hidden in shadows, and so he rose quietly and moved away from the fire ring.

He'd dreamed of the birds that night, of their nests in the roof of the world. He'd dreamed that one of the birds had flown to him and given him its beak full of manna, which was good to eat. Were they real, he wondered? Did the old blind man speak the truth about the birds?

He wandered past the first wall of the ruins, farther into darkness, where he could see the brilliant stars shining in the dome of the sky. He wanted to move out beyond the ruins, but when he gazed across the road he only saw the darkness, the shadows of ill-defined hills, and silhouettes of scrawny trees. Anything could be waiting in the shadows, patiently watching to see if he came out just a little farther—

Tam kept his place by the wall. But he gazed up at the stars again and tried to see the wings of the night birds flying from the celestial eaves. He wondered, if he called out loudly enough, would the birds hear him, and bring down enough manna for them all to eat? But he wouldn't call out, he couldn't. He would wake the others, or wake the attention of something dangerous hiding in the world beyond the ruins.

He also worried if he called out, no birds would come. It was better this way, to think of the beautiful night birds on the roof of the world, than to know that it was just a story, just a lie. In the infinite darkness beyond the ruins lay something else; perhaps it was watching him now, waiting, or preparing to move toward him. Why didn't it come? And why was he so afraid of it?

Tam turned. The dog stood behind him, watching him closely. "Go away," he whispered, but the dog ignored him.

Tam walked back inside the ruins, lay by Keira, and soon fell asleep again.

Tam woke to the sound of the ugly girl crying in heaving sobs that were terrible to hear. He lifted his head and gazed around the ruins, trying to understand what he was seeing, and then he knew. The Uncle was kneeling over Keira, but not to rouse her, or give her water. He was slowly folding her small body into one of the blankets, covering her reverently. Lauren knelt nearby, holding her scarf to her face as she cried.

Tam rose to his feet, a heaviness pressing down on his shoulders and moving into his chest.

The old blind man stood behind the Uncle, reciting a benediction as his voice broke with sadness. Even the brothers wiped tears from their eyes with the backs of their hands, because Keira had been a beautiful little girl, and her voice, when it was still in her body, had been a voice that filled their world with joy.

The Uncle made a terrible noise in his throat, as if gasping for air, and held his hands to his face a moment before releasing it again and regaining his composure. He inhaled deeply, then spread his arms to everyone, and everyone watched him expectantly.

"Our beautiful child has left us," he said, as if each of his words had been wrested from his throat forcibly. "Let us come together, and mourn her passing."

Tam moved toward the Uncle, as did Lauren, and the brothers, and the old blind man. When they stood together, the Uncle spoke again.

"She's gone," he said, "but she still carries our love with her to the life beyond this one. She will never be hungry or thirsty again. She has made her journey to paradise."

Tam was glad the Uncle said these words; the Uncle was a pious man, a good man, and he made certain that everyone in their group was pious, too. Tam hoped to be as pious as the Uncle when he was grown.

"Before we build a fire to prepare her body," the Uncle said, "let us kneel and give thanks to all those who have gone before her. Let us praise all those who have sacrificed their lives to give us our life's bread and help us continue on our journey."

Tam knelt, closed his eyes, and tried to pray, because he was truly thankful that nothing had come into the camp from the shadows in the night. But the mention of bread brought the night birds back to his mind, so he had a difficult time finding the right words to give thanks.

He saw the great black wings spread out against the night sky as the birds flew majestically, the manna dripping from their beaks—*bless Graham, and Samantha, and Nona*—he saw them sleeping in their great nests, too, waiting for the moon to rise—*bless Kay, and Lawson, and the old beggar*—one day he would call up to them, just to see, just to know, he really would—*bless Emil, and Innes, and the man who couldn't speak*—perhaps, too, he would climb on the back of one of the great birds and fly with it to the roof of the world—*bless Leticia, and Mama, and Papa, and pretty baby Beth—*

REVIEWS

In the Wake of Old Time

a column by John Michael Greer

Davy
Ballantine, 1964

&

The Judgement of Eve
Simon & Schuster, 1966

The Company of Glory
Pyramid, 1975

Still I Persist in Wondering
Dell, 1978

all written by
Edgar Pangborn

ONE OF THE THINGS I HOPE readers and writers of deindustrial science fiction (SF) will keep in mind, as our genre (or sub-genre, or sub-sub-genre) proceeds on its merry way, is that a great deal of first-rate deindustrial SF has already seen print. The moniker may be new—to the best of my recollection, I coined the term "deindustrial SF" myself in 2014—but speculative fiction that explores the decline and fall of industrial society, and the futures that might come after? That's just about as old as science fiction itself.

I want to stress the words "decline and fall" here, because it's very common these days to lump deindustrial SF together with the far more popular field of post-apocalyptic SF. Though there's a surface similarity to the two—after all, both deal with the end of industrial society and what, if anything, comes next—the underlying assumptions of the two genres stand in flat opposition to one another. Like most other branches of the burgeoning tree of science fiction, post-apocalyptic SF assumes that industrial society is the normal, natural, and inescapable endpoint of human social evolution. That's why some humongous catastrophe or other has to be dragged into the story to get rid of industrial society, at least for a while, and that's why, in story after story after story, what comes after apocalypse is inevitably an attempt to rebuild a new industrial society on the pattern of the old.

That's not just found in the bargain-basement level of post-apocalyptic SF, either. Consider Walter M. Miller's *A Canticle for Leibowitz*, a major SF novel by any measure, and one of the seminal post-apocalyptic SF tales. In Miller's vision, what follows our civilization's suicide by mushroom cloud is a trip right back up the familiar ladder of progress: the first part of his novel is set in a rerun of the Middle Ages, the second in a rerun of the Age of Reason, and the third in a rerun of the late twentieth century people in Miller's time expected to witness, complete with space travel—and another round of nuclear weapons. It makes for a great story, but absent from Miller's vision is any sense that our kind of progress, leading to our kind of society, might be something other than a one-way street to our kind of future.

Thus it's all the more remarkable that *A Canticle for Leibowitz* inspired, by way of counterblast, one of the great works of deindustrial SF: Edgar Pangborn's *Davy*.

The main point of dispute between Miller and Pangborn wasn't the shape of the future. Miller was a Roman Catholic, and much of his story revolved around the Catholic Church as a force for good in postapocalyptic times. For his part, Pangborn was a gay man who had seen all too much of the bigoted and condemnatory side of American Christian religiosity; he was accordingly an atheist, and the role of religion in his imagined future is relentlessly negative—for him, as for his viewpoint characters, religion can be defined as ignorance defended by Inquisition. Still, what might have started out as a mere antireligious screed projected onto the future succeeded in becoming something far deeper and more impressive.

A good deal of that has to do with the writing. Pangborn was a first-rate writer with a gift for prose that's rarely been equaled in science fiction. He told *Davy* entirely in the slangy, bawdy, rollicking first-person voice of the title character, and it works brilliantly. The novel presents itself as Davy's own autobiography, laboriously penned during the otherwise empty hours as he and his companions sail out into the Atlantic. Readers of mine who find this reminiscent of my novel *Star's Reach* aren't wrong; some aspects of my tale, including the first-person narrative and the jumbled timeline, were a deliberate homage to Pangborn's. But all things considered, *Davy* is the better novel of the two.

Davy himself? He's the child of a harlot in a second-rate whorehouse in the stockaded town of Skoar in the little nation of Moha, which you'll find in what's now upstate New York about four hundred years after the end of what he calls Old Time, and we call the modern industrial world. As an orphan, and not a particularly well-behaved one, he faces a lifetime of slavery, so he runs off to the wilderness, falls in with a handful of deserters from Moha's army, then finds a home among the Ramblers, who are something like a cross between a Romany caravan and a traveling carnival. Eventually he finds his way to the coastal nation of Nuin, where a scientific and technological renaissance briefly struggles to life, and then gets stomped by the forces of political reaction and religious bigotry.

Across that armature of events runs Davy's own slow journey toward maturity and understanding—*Davy* is among other things a coming-of-age novel, or if you want to be all formal and German about it, a *Bildungsroman*—as well as the trajectories of half a dozen other major characters, each of them capably rendered. For the connoisseur of deindustrial SF, though, another trajectory may be of even more interest, and that is the way Davy's world has shaken itself out in the wake of Old Time.

Pangborn's grasp of history rivals that of anyone else in the deindustrial-SF field then or now, and his take on the downfall of Old Time—seen only in glimpses here and there in *Davy*—displays this with effortless grace. There was a nuclear war, though it wasn't the be-all and end-all of everything, just one major incident in the long slide into the Years of Confusion. There was an epidemic, recalled dimly in Davy's time as the Red Plague. Then the seas rose and the climate of what's now New England and the mid-Atlantic states turned semitropical: yes, Pangborn was already there back in the 1960s, when scientists were still debating whether the immediate future held a hothouse earth or a new ice age.

Over the course of the Years of Confusion, the human population of eastern North America dropped to a few percent of its Old Time peak, and the technological and cultural level of the survivors lurched unsteadily downward to various points along a spectrum between tribal hunter-gatherers and agricultural peasants, with health problems, social structures, illiteracy, and superstitions to match. Wilderness pressed close around the scattered settlements, with wolves and tigers a constant menace. (The latter, as Davy learns in the course of his wanderings, are descended from animals in zoos set free in the last years of Old Time.) Rates of live birth and infant mortality stayed respectively low and high for the usual reasons, and the nuclear foolishness of an earlier age meant that a certain number of the offspring were mues—mutants, in the language of Old Time—who were customarily killed at birth.

That was the raw material out of which Davy's world slowly emerged. A religious institution—the Holy Murcan Church, whose prophet Abraham perished on the wheel not long after the end of Old Time—provided the glue that held the nascent society together. Though Pangborn portrays it in terms he lifted directly from the standard American Protestant parody of medieval Catholicism, he also shows glimpses of its more constructive sides as well. In the usual way, trade springs up between communities, ships begin poking their way up and down the northeastern seaboard and through the new waterways opened up by sea level rise, literacy becomes less unheard-of, if not yet common, and the scattered communities of survivors coalesce into new nations.

It's another mark of Pangborn's grasp of history that these aren't the generic medieval baronies that have been so overused in deindustrial and post-apocalyptic SF. Tunics and cloaks, straight swords with cross hilts, and the rest of the hardware made all but inescapable by J.R.R. Tolkien and the busy industry of derivative neomedieval fantasy that paddled along gamely in his titanic wake—Pangborn recognized that those were the hallmarks of one specific dark age, not of dark ages in general. The little deindustrial nations through which *Davy* wends its way are thus their own kind of dark age states. Here's how Davy himself described them:

"Now I think of it, every nation I know of except Nuber is a great democracy. The exception, Nuber the Holy City, is not really a nation anyway, just a few square miles of sanctified topsoil facing the Hudson Sea, enclosed on its other three sides by some of Katskil's mountains. It is the spiritual capital of the world, in other words the terrestrial site of that heavenly contraption the Holy Murcan Church. . . . Katskil itself is a kingdom. Nuin is a commonwealth, with a hereditary presidency of absolute powers. Levannon is a kingdom, but governed by a Board of Trade. Lomeda and the other Low Countries are ecclesiastical states, the boss panjandrum being called a Prince Cardinal. Rhode, Vairmant, and Penn are republics; Conicut's a kingdom; Bershar is mostly a mess. But they're all great democracies, and I hope this will grow clearer to you one day when the ocean is less wet."

Notice how the phrase "great democracy" functions in Davy's time the way that the political tropes of the Roman world functioned in ninth-century Europe. Charlemagne was a Roman emperor in exactly the same sense that the kingdom of Katskil is a great democracy, and it's typical of Pangborn that he was able to weave that into his story with so little apparent effort. Equally typical, and equally skillful, is the way that Pangborn points up the deeply equivocal nature of Old Time as seen from Davy's perspective, as a source of lost treasures of knowledge and of constantly present burdens and horrors.

As a novel, a coming-of-age story, and an exploration of the kind of future we might actually get, *Davy* is a triumph, and belongs on any well-stocked bookshelf of deindustrial SF.

Pangborn went on to write two more novels and a flurry of short stories set in the same future *Davy* painted so vividly. Both novels and most of the stories are set before the time of Davy, and provide a good deal of the backstory. *The Judgment of Eve* is set a few decades after the One-Day War and the Red Plague; it's frankly more a post-apocalyptic novel than a deindustrial one. Its plot is a little contrived: Eve Newman and her mother are the only two people still alive in what was once the town of East Redfield and is now a makeshift farm surrounded by newborn forest. To the farm come three men, fleeing from the narrow-minded religious community of Shelter Town, following the dream of founding a new and less dour settlement somewhere else. All three of them, of course, promptly fall in love with Eve, and her way of making a choice among them is to send each of them alone into the wilderness for a year, with instructions to come back with an answer to her question: what is love? It sounds rather corny and in places it is; the allegory gets a little thick at times, too, though Pangborn's lively writing and his compelling portrait of the nearly empty landscape of the Northeast do much to salvage the tale and make it worth reading.

The Company of Glory is also placed early in the years after Old Time, within living memory of the One-Day War, and it's set in the town of Nuber—the same Nuber that would become the headquarters of the Holy Murcan Church by Davy's time. In this story it's a crowded, lively little town where a few old people still remember industrial civilization and one of them, the storyteller Demetrios, weaves memories of Old Time into his tales of wonder. Not all of his stories deal with the world that's passed away; he also witnessed the execution of Abraham on the wheel, the event that ultimately gave rise to the Holy Murcan Church, and his insistence on repeating that story at a time when the political authorities of Nuber would much rather see it suppressed gets him thrown into jail.

A group of his friends break him out of the ramshackle prison, and join Demetrios in a journey west through a landscape just beginning to recover from deindustrial collapse. The little group attracts others and grows into a company in the old sense of the word, a band of companions—the Company of Glory—and the glory in question is a vision of a human community guided by love instead of organized stupidity. The notion, new and fashionable in science fiction back then, that jealousy-free pansexuality was the solution to all the world's problems plays much the same role in *The Company of Glory* that it does in some of Robert Heinlein's later and less satisfactory novels; as with *The Judgment of Eve*, the allegory gets a little thick, especially at the end. Even so, it's a lively, funny, thoughtful read, and deserves more attention than it's had—though the same can be said for everything Pangborn wrote.

There remain the short stories set in Davy's world, many of which are still scattered among back issues of science fiction magazines and anthologies long out of print. The one anthology I know of, *Still I Persist In Wondering*, collects seven of them. They range in quality from good to stunningly good; the final story, "The Night Wind," is a prose poem on love and liberation as brilliant as anything in science fiction. Some of the stories that didn't make it into the collection are to my mind at least as good, and it would be welcome, to use no stronger word, if some publisher were able to contact whoever holds his copyrights today, and make arrangements for a complete anthology of the tales he set in the wake of Old Time. All in all, Edgar Pangborn set a very high bar for the writer of deindustrial SF, and his work in the genre deserves many readings.

Addendum:

In future issues of *Into the Ruins*, I plan on continuing this column and surveying the desolate but enticing landscapes portrayed by past authors of deindustrial SF. While I have a good many books already lined up to review, there's doubtless no shortage of stories of that kind that I haven't read or don't remember. If you have favorites you'd like to propose for review, or for that matter really dreadful examples of the species, by all means drop me a note c/o Into the Ruins at joel@intotheruins.com, or by mail at:

Figuration Press
3515 SE Clinton Street
Portland, OR 97202

Many thanks!

- John Michael Greer
thearchdruidreport.blogspot.com

Restoring Harmony
by Joëlle Anthony

G.P. Putnam's Sons, 2010

THE IDEA OF COLLAPSE is gaining greater traction in the news media these days. Streaming infotainment of the ongoing convergence of crises is for now accessed with ease via digital media. Print newsstands, like the one my grandpa raised his family of six on, have for the most part disappeared (but are in sore need of a reboot). Meanwhile, in the world of fiction, accounts of collapse have been trickling into the outskirts of mainstream publishing. For the most part these bypass the nuclear meltdown scenarios that populated science fiction in the Cold War era and instead deal with ecolo-gical, economic or social concerns. As an employee in the catalog department of a large library system I get to see a lot of new releases and it seems to me that books confronting some aspect of collapse head-on tend to be in the young adult market. From my vantage point, books aimed at teens have greater leeway and freedom in addressing the kinds of day-to-day survival concerns that are becoming prevalent in a world marked with limited access to energy, health care, and other resources. I find it troubling that a much larger portion of the fiction spectrum is made up of realistic literary novels written for adults by graduates of bloated MFA programs, whose characters and plots don't appear to be affected by actual realities but are sucked into the black hole of terminal navel gazing. They aren't the kind of books that do much to prepare people for the steep road ahead.

Hard work is in store for all who are engaged in a meaningful response to the crises now facing humanity. When physical, intellectual and emotional muscles are all under strain from Herculean labors, a harvest of fresh fruits and veggies are necessary to supply the body with proper nutrients. *Restoring Harmony* is a vegetable garden of a book whose raised beds are made up of the kind of nourishing staples that have become part of the ongoing conversation of collapse. In 2041 oil has run out, fragile governments have fallen apart and the situation worldwide is one marked by chaos. Sixteen year old Molly McClure has it better than most. A farm girl and musician hailing from an island in British Columbia, her rural community has for the most part been isolated from the destruction caused by the unraveling of society on the mainland. With the island doctor dead after an accident, and her mother's pregnancy compromised, she is sent on a mission to Portland, Oregon to retrieve her estranged grandfather, himself a man of medicine, and her grandma who has suffered from a stroke. With only an almanac and her trusty fiddle Jewels as companions, she sneaks across the border into Seattle.

As is typical of many coming-of-age stories the heroine of the tale is confronted early on with her own naïveté. She shows her unfamiliarity with paper currency while buying a ticket to Portland at a train station, and soon after arriving in Oregon is already broke. In an attempt to earn back some of her lost funds and buy some food for her underfed grandparents, she busks at a local market, not knowing it's run by an organized crime outfit who expects a cut. As much as her fiddle seems to bring people joy, it also gets her into trouble. Yet her music is her lifeline, her life blood, a way for her to relieve stress and center herself in the harsh social environment of a crumbling suburbia.

One of Molly's challenges is to convince her grandpa to come back to Canada with her. This is no easy task

as he still resents Molly's mom for having skipped college to become an organic farmer. Yet he can barely keep a volunteer tomato going and relies on the kindness of his alcoholic neighbor throwing produce over the fence to stay fed. Molly grows her confidence by taking over the neighbor's weedy garden, whipping it into shape and canning the produce for the approaching cold season. As grandpa's belly gets filled, his heart opens up, and he begins to see the value of the unschooled skills his daughter has instilled in his grandchild.

The novel's love interest subplot is well-cobbled and doesn't overshadow the other elements of the story. On arriving in Portland, Molly meets a slightly older young man who later brings her a gift of deer skin shoes he made himself to replace the ones she lost on the train. Riding his bike over to her grandparents place, he brings some other gifts around, as well as protection. She comes to realize that his protection, and his access to rare goods, though well-intentioned, comes from him being an up and coming member of the local mob. How he disentangles himself from organized crime, and how she gets two elders and two orphaned children back across the border put their combined skills to the test.

The novel *Restoring Harmony* was the quite the reward, as it spun a yarn that is a reliable guide through the strange labyrinths of collapse. It takes common coming-of-age and falling-in-love young adult tropes and uses them to create a hook catchy as a pop song. The strength of the book is in all the macro and micro details of what life will tend to look like in a society breaking at the seams: unreliable bridges and infrastructure in dangerous states of decay, outbreaks of polio, increased border tensions between the U.S. and Canada, squatters in the suburbs, orphans and alcoholism.

I am glad teens are being exposed to books such as *Restoring Harmony*, a novel that grapples with the predicaments of our age without sugar coating solutions. I hope that it inspires those who read it to pick up a shovel, learn to play an instrument, or take on the task of learning a useful skill or trade. These forms of embodied knowledge will be useful for achieving harmony in life, even as chaos rages outside the door.

- Justin Patrick Moore
sothismedia.com

STATIC ON A QUIET NIGHT
BY JOEL CARIS

a very short excerpt

Shuffling across the living room in exhausted, threadbare night clothes, Ali dropped heavy into the torn but overstuffed recliner, sighing as her body settled. Just enough moonlight crept in from the room's large, south-facing windows to outline her corner: the chair she sat in, the small table next to her and the radio upon it, tied into the house's solitary power source—a small wind generator bolted on the roof, whispering a rhythmic *whump-whump-whump* above her in the steady wind sweeping across the plains to which she and her house belonged. After a few moments of customary quiet and the stray, fleeting thoughts it so often brought, she switched on the radio. A soft and steady static filled the room.

As she fiddled with the tuning dial, the static gave way to a man's voice, soft and steady itself, so familiar to her. She eased back at his company and closed her eyes, conjuring her usual image of his face despite the fact she had never laid eyes on him. Brown hair, a wide nose, and a softness to his features belying the death and loss that unwound behind him, stretching four years into the past. She had been with him all four of those years, suffering her own losses, listening to his stories and aching when his voice cracked. She cried when he lost his boy. She cried when he reminisced of his wife. She cried when he spoke of the beauty of the world, and nodded when he spoke of its needs.

"It's the wind tonight," he said, his words cracked in the ragged reception. "The way it moves over the land, across the rocky outcroppings and through the trees, stirring the dust and always whispering to me." The radio hissed quiet a moment, broken only by a stray breath. She imagined him with closed eyes, listening for the whispers. He always spoke halting but rhythmic, never scared to let a silence spread out around him. So many years ago, in her early childhood, she remembered the frantic nature of the radio—of all media—and the way silence never could be allowed. You lost people in silence. They couldn't bear the thoughts that came with it. But now it was everywhere, and so often the thoughts were all that kept the loneliness at bay.

"That's what speaks to me," he said. "Tonight it's the wind."

After a moment she thought, *But it's never silent.* Birds, insects, the scrabble of rodents. Coyotes screaming and yipping across the night, always eager to make claim. The livestock on the land. The wind and, occasionally, even rain. Even the snow. The snow was silent, but not really. Snow always brought the loudest silence, deafening across the landscape. The motors, though—God, she could remember all the motors. She rarely heard them now. In the cities still, of course, but not so much out here in the country. It had been a long time since anyone came to visit her by car. Not many came other than Franklin, and he always came by horse or foot, clomping one way or another—those big damn shitkicker boots of his so loud on her wooden porch. "Christ, Franklin, I could hear you coming from Idaho those boots are so goddamn loud," she would tell him, leaning in the doorway. He always replied, a touch indignant, that they had never touched such awful land. She didn't understand what he had against Idaho; her time there thirty years prior had been pleasant enough, made best by her meeting Crag. That hadn't lasted long, but god what a time she had with him.

"Tonight I need to tell a story," the radio said, bringing her back. "I have thought and thought and thought. And I have listened. I have listened to so many of this land's words, and it's time to pass its story on." A cough, and then a sigh, the static crackling through them both. She could almost place its rhythm with the wind, the steady *whump* of the wind turbine above her, but probably she only imagined it. "It's a story of deprivation and hunger. It's a story of human failing and blindness. It's a story of the amends we must make." His face, the softness, brown hair and brown skin and now a rigidity—she could see it—hardening across the softness as he brought forth his lesson. "It's a story about how hungry this land is and why it continues to take our children, our husbands and wives, our brothers and sisters." She nodded. Oh yes, she knew this story, though she wanted to hear how he would tell it.

"It's a story," he said, "of—"

Made in the USA
San Bernardino, CA
12 March 2017